A telescope swings on its clockwork mounting. Sudden shapes move in its field . . . an alarm is tripped and a siren skirls into the quiet air . . .

There were eight of them, walking steadily toward the camp. It was too far yet to see details, but sunlight flashed hard off metal . . .

The siren rose to a new note: Alarm stations! General Alert!

. . . Lorenzen bit his lip. "Seems to be a half dozen or so coming on foot. What the hell are we s-s-scared of?"

In truth the aliens did not seem terribly dangerous, with their hatchets and muzzle-loading smooth-bores—but the previous Troas Expedition had never returned; it was all too likely that these furred beings were the cause . . .

"The shock at the end, after the action, when you suddenly realize that you've been cheering the wrong side, or the weaklings aren't, or some basic law has been ignored . . . the color, smell, taste of an alien world, a nonhuman society, a globular cluster or the universe seen from the very edge of lightspeed . . . these things Poul shows better than anyone."

—Larry Niven

QUESTION
AND
ANSWER

by
POUL ANDERSON

ace books
A Division of Charter Communications Inc.
A GROSSET & DUNLAP COMPANY
1120 Avenue of the Americas
New York, New York 10036

QUESTION AND ANSWER

Introduction

Nowadays specialized science fiction anthologies are everywhere, often filled with stories written just for those books. Robots, time travel, dystopias, telepathy, female authors—the themes are multitudinous, leading Vonda McIntyre once to imagine a volume called *Dwarf Stars: Stories by Short Science Fiction Writers*. A quarter century ago, this kind of thing was unheard of. It sufficed that a tale fit within the genre (whatever that means; there are as many definitions of this field as there have been people trying to define it).

The present yarn grew out of a pioneering attempt to create a common starting point, if not a common motif. The planet Troas was designed by a professional scientist to seem attractively Earth-like, though with some exotic features. It had one catch. The first expedition to it never came back. Three writers, Isaac Asimov, James Blish, and myself, were given this much and asked to proceed at length. As might have been expected, the works we produced were wildly different. Unfortunately, plans fell through for their publication in a single volume, and they came out separately over a considerable period of time.

Mine was serialized in *Astounding,* as today's *Analog* was then called, and afterward appeared in paperback under the title *Planet of No Return*. I have here restored the original name. Otherwise I have made no changes, not even in the orbit of Troas, the stability of which has been challenged. Planet-building is a lot of fun—could that be why God has seemingly done it so often?—and the risk of being caught out, which we mortals run when we play at it, simply adds zest to the game.

—Poul Anderson

"Wisdom is better than strength; nevertheless the poor man's wisdom is despised, and his words are not heard. The words of wise men are heard in quiet more than the cry of him that ruleth among fools. Wisdom is better than weapons of war: but one sinner destroyeth much good."

—Ecclesiastes, ix, 16-18

CHAPTER I

SOMEWHERE A RELAY clicked, and somewhere else a robot muttered to itself. Alarm lights shot through the spectrum into a hot and angry red, flashing and flashing, and a siren began its idiotic hoot.

"Get *out* of here!"

Three of the techs dropped what they were doing and shoved for a purchase against the nearest wall. The contrόl panel was a yammer of crimson. Their weightless bodies slammed through the siren-raddled air toward the door.

"Come back here, you—!" They were gone before Kemal Gummus-lugil's roar was finished. He spat after them and grabbed a hand ring and pushed himself toward the panel.

Radiation, radiation, radiation, screamed the siren. Radiation enough to blaze through all shielding and come out with a fury that ionized the engine-room air and turned the alarm system crazy. But the effects were cumulative— Gummus-lugil got close enough to the meters to read them. The intensity was mounting, but he could stand half an hour of it without danger.

1

Why had they saddled him with a bunch of thumbfingered morons so superstitious about gamma rays that they fled when the converter gave them a hard look?

He extended his arms before him, stopping his free-fall speed with fingertips and triceps. Reaching out for the manual cut-off, he slapped it down with a clank. Somehow the automatic safeties had failed to operate, and the nuclear fires in the converter were turning it into a small sun—but hell dammit, a man could still stop the thing!

Other relays went to work. Baffle plates shot home, cutting off the fuel supply. The converter's power output was shunted to the generators, building up the damper fields which should stop the reaction—

And didn't!

It took seconds for Gummus-lugil to realize that fact. Around him, within him, the air was full of death; to an eye sensitive in the hard frequencies, his lungs must have glowed; but now the intensity should be dropping, the nuclei slowed in fighting the damper field till their speed dropped below resonance, and he could stop to find out what was wrong. He pulled his way along the giant panel toward the meters for the automatic safeties, and felt sweat prickling under his arms.

He and his crew had been testing the newly installed converter, nothing more. Something could have been wrong with one or another of the parts; but the immense complex of interlocking controls which was the engine's governor should have been self-regulating, foolproof, and—

The siren began hooting still louder.

Gummus-lugil felt his whole body grow wet. The fuel supply had been cut off, yes, but the reaction hadn't been stopped. No damper fields! Behind the casing, all the fires of hell were burning themselves out. It would take hours before that was done, and everybody who stayed on the ship would be a dead man.

For an instant he hung there, aware of the endless falling sensation of weightlessness, aware of the noise and the vicious red lights. If they abandoned the ship in her orbit, she would be hot for days to come and the converter would be ruined. He had to flush the thing—now!

Behind him, the shielded bulkheads closed, and the ventilation system stopped its steady whirr. The ship's robomonitors would not let poison spread too swiftly through her entire body. They, at least, were still functioning. But they didn't care about him, and radiation was eating at his flesh.

He bit his teeth together and got to work. The emergency manuals still seemed okay. He spoke into his throat mike: "Gummus-lugil to bridge. I'm going to flush this damned thing. That means the outside hull will be hot for a few hours. Anybody out there?"

"No." The supervisor's voice sounded small and scared. "We're all standing by the lifeboat locks. Don't you think we should just abandon ship and let her burn herself out?"

"And ruin a billion solars' worth of engine? No, thanks! Just stay where you are, you'll be okay." Even in this moment, the engineer snorted. He began turning the main flushing wheel, bracing his feet against his body's tendency to rotate the other way.

The auxiliaries were purely mechanical and hydraulic—for which praises be to the designers, now when all electronic equipment seemed to have gone mad. Gummus-lugil grunted, feeling the effort in his muscles. A series of ports opened. The rage of more-than-incandescent gases spilled out into space, a brief flame against darkness and then nothing the human eye could see.

Slowly, the red lights dulled to yellow and the siren moderated its voice. The radioactivity in the engine room was falling off already. Gummus-lugil decided that he'd not had a harmful dose, though the doctors would probably order him a couple of months off the job.

He went through the special safety exit; in the chamber beyond, he shucked his clothes and gave them to the robot. Beyond that, there were three successive decontamination rooms; it took half an hour before a Geiger proclaimed him fit for human society. He slipped on the coverall which another robot handed him and made his way to the bridge.

The supervisor shrank from him, just a trifle, as he entered. "All right," said Gummus-lugil sarcastically. "I know I'm a little radioactive yet. I know I should go ringing a bell and crying, 'Unclean! Unclean!' But right now I want to make a call to Earth.''

"Huh . . . oh, yes, yes. Of course." The supervisor scurried through the air toward the com-desk. "Where to?"

"Lagrange Institute head office."

"What . . . went wrong? Do you know?"

"Everything. More than could possibly happen by chance. If I hadn't been the only man aboard with the brains of an oyster, the ship would've been abandoned and the converter ruined."

"You don't mean—"

Gummus-lugil raised his fingers and ticked them off one by one: " S, A, B, O, T, A, G, E spells 'sabotage.' And I want to get the bastard that did it and hang him with his own guts."

CHAPTER II

JOHN LORENZEN was looking out of his hotel window when the call came. He was on the 58th floor, and the sheer drop down made him feel a little dizzy. They didn't build that high on Luna.

Below him, above him, around him, the city was like a jungle, airy flex-bridges looping from one slim tower to the next; and it glowed and burned with light, further out than he could see, over the curve of the world. The white and gold and red and royal blue illumination wasn't continuous; here and there a wide patch of black showed a park, with a fountain of fire or glowing water in the middle of its night; but the lights reached for many kilometers. Quito never slept.

It was near midnight, when a lot of rockets would be taking off. Lorenzen wanted to see the sight; it was famous in the Solar System. He had paid double price for a room facing the wall of the spaceport, not without twinges of conscience, for the Lagrange Institute was footing the bills, but he'd done it. A boyhood on a remote Alaskan farm, a long grind through college—the poor student going through on scholarships and

6

assistantships—and then the years at Luna Observatory, hadn't held anything like this. He wasn't complaining about his life, but it hadn't been anything very spectacular either, and if now he was to go into the great darkness beyond the sun, he ought to see Quito Spaceport at midnight first. He might not have another chance.

The 'phone chimed gently. He started, swearing at his own nervousness. There wasn't anything to be scared of. They wouldn't bite him. But the palms of his hands were wet.

He stepped over and thumbed the switch. "Hello," he said.

A face grew in the screen. It wasn't a particularly memorable face—smooth, plump, snub-nosed, thin gray hair—and the body seemed short and stout. The voice was rather high but not unpleasant, speaking in North American English: "Dr. Lorenzen?"

"Yes. Who . . . is this, please?" In Lunopolis, everybody knew everybody else, and trips to Leyport and Ciudad Libre had been rare. Lorenzen wasn't used to this welter of strangers.

And he wasn't used to Earth gravity or changeable weather or the thin cool air of Ecuador. He felt lost.

"Avery. Edward Avery. I'm with the government, but also with the Lagrange Institute—sort of liaison man between the two, and I'll be going along on the expedition as psychomed. Hope I didn't get you out of bed?"

7

"No . . . no, not at all. I'm used to irregular hours. You get that way on Luna."

"And in Quito too—believe me." Avery grinned. "Look, could you come over and see me?"

"I . . . well . . . now?"

"As good a time as any, if you aren't busy. We can have a few drinks, maybe, and talk a little. I was supposed to approach you anyway, while you were in town."

"Well . . . well, yes, sure, I suppose so." Lorenzen felt rushed off his feet. After the leisurely years on the Moon, he couldn't adapt to this pace they had on Earth. He wanted to spit in somebody's eye and tell him they'd go at his, Lorenzen's, speed for a change; but he knew he never would.

"Good, fine. Thanks a lot." Avery gave him the address and switched off.

A low rumble murmured through the room. The rockets! Lorenzen hurried back to the window and saw the shielding wall like the edge of the world, black against their light. One, two, three, a dozen metal spears rushing upward on flame and thunder, and the Moon a cool shield high above the city—yes, it was worth seeing.

He dialed for an aircab and slipped a cloak over his thin lounging pajamas. The 'copter appeared in minutes, hovering just beyond his balcony and extending a gangway. He walked in, feeling his cloak grow warm as it sucked power from the 'cast system, and sat down and punched out the address he wanted.

"Dos solarios y cincuenta centos, por favor."

The mechanical voice made him feel embarrassed; he barely stopped himself from apologizing as he put a tenner in the slot. The autopilot gave him his change as the cab swung into the sky.

He was set off at another hotel—apparently Avery didn't live permanently in Quito either—and made his way down the hall to the suite named. "Lorenzen," he said to the door, and it opened for him. He walked into an anteroom, giving his cloak to the robot, and was met by Avery himself.

Yes, the psychman was pretty short. Lorenzen looked down from his own gaunt height as he shook hands. He was only about half Avery's age, he guessed—a tall skinny young man who didn't quite know where to put his feet, unkempt brown hair, gray eyes, blunt homely features with the smooth even tan of Lunar sun-type fluoros.

"Very glad you could come, Dr. Lorenzen." Avery looked guilty and lowered his voice to a whisper. "Afraid I can't offer you that drink right now. We've got another expedition man here—came over on business . . . a Martian, you know—"

"Huh?" Lorenzen caught himself just in time. He didn't know if he'd like having a Martian for crewmate, but it was too late now.

They entered the living room. The third man

was already seated, and did not rise for them. He was also tall and lean, but with a harshness to his outlines that the tight black clothes of a Noachian Dissenter did not help; his face was all angles; jutting nose and chin, hard black eyes under the close-cropped dark hair.

"Joab Thornton—John Lorenzen—please sit down." Avery lowered himself into a chair. Thornton sat stiffly on the edge of his, obviously disliking the idea of furniture which molded itself to his contours.

"Dr. Thornton is a physicist—radiation and optics—at the University of New Zion," explained Avery. "Dr. Lorenzen is with the observatory at Lunopolis. Both you gentlemen will be going to Lagrange with us, of course. You might as well get acquainted now." He tried to smile.

"Thornton—haven't I heard your name in connection with x-ray photography?" asked Lorenzen. "We've used some of your results to examine the hard spectra of stars, I believe. Very valuable."

"Thank you." The Martian's lips creased upward. "The credit is not to me but to the Lord." There didn't seem to be any answer for that.

"Excuse me." He turned to Avery. "I want to get this over with, and they said you were the expedition's official wailing wall. I've just been looking over the personnel list and checking up on the records. You have one engineer down by the name of Reuben Young. His religion—if you can call it that—is New Christian."

"Ummm . . . yes—" Avery dropped his eyes. "I know your sect doesn't get along with his, but—"

"Doesn't get along!" A vein pulsed in Thornton's temple. "The New Christians forced us to migrate to Mars when they were in power. It was they who perverted doctrine till all Reformism was a stink in the nostrils of the people. It was they who engineered our war with Venus." (Not so, thought Lorenzen: part of it had been power rivalry, part of it the work of Terrestrial psychmen who wanted their masters to play Kilkenny cat.) "It is still they who slander us to the rest of the Solar System. It is their fanatics who make it necessary for me to carry a gun here on Earth." He gulped and clenched his fists. When he spoke again, it was quietly:

"I am not an intolerant man. Only the Almighty knows the just from the unjust. You can have as many Jews, Catholics, Moslems, unbelievers, collectivists, Sebastianists, and I know not what else along as you choose. But by joining the expedition I take on myself an obligation: to work with, and perhaps to fight with and save the life of, everyone else aboard. I cannot assume this obligation toward a New Christian.

"If Young goes along, I don't. That's all."

"Well—well—" Avery ran a hand through his hair, an oddly helpless gesture. "Well, I'm sorry you feel that way—"

"Those idiots in the government supposedly running our personnel office for us should have known it from the start."

"You wouldn't consider—"

"I wouldn't. You have two days to inform me that Young has been discharged; thereafter I book passage back to Mars."

Thornton got up. "I'm sorry to be so rude about it," he finished, "but that's the way it is. Speak to the office for me. I'd better be going now." He shook Lorenzen's hand. "Glad to have met you, sir. I hope the next time will be under better conditions. I'd like to ask you about some of that x-ray work."

When he was gone, Avery sighed gustily. "How about that drink? I need one bad myself. What an off-orbit!"

"From the realistic point of view," said Lorenzen cautiously, "he was right. There'd have been murder if those two were on the same ship."

"I suppose so." Avery picked up the chair mike and spoke to the RoomServ. Turning back to his guest: "How that slip-up occurred, I don't know. But it doesn't surprise me. There seems to be a curse on the whole project. Everything's gone wrong. We're a year behind our original schedule, and it's cost almost twice the estimate."

The RoomServ discharged a tray with two whiskies and soda; it landed on the roller table, which came over to the men. Avery picked up his glass and drank thirstily. "Young will have to go," he said. "He's just an engineer, plenty more where he came from; we need a physicist of Thornton's caliber."

"It's strange," said Lorenzen, "that a man so brilliant in his line—he's a top-flight mathematician too, you know—should be a . . . Dissenter."

"Not strange." Avery sipped moodily. "The human mind is a weird and tortuous thing. It's perfectly possible to believe in a dozen mutually contradictory things at once. Few people ever really learn how to think at all; those who do, think only with the surface of their minds. The rest is still conditioned reflex and rationalization of a thousand subconscious fears and hates and longings. We're finally getting a science of man—a *real* science; we're finally learning how a child must be brought up if he is to be truly sane. But it'll take a long time before the results show on any large scale. There is so much insanity left over from all our history, so much built into the very structure of human society."

"Well—" Lorenzen shifted uneasily. "I daresay you're right. But, uh, about the business at hand—you wanted to see me—"

"Just for a drink and a talk," said Avery. "It's my business to get to know every man on the ship better than he knows himself. But that'll also take time."

"You have my psych-tests from when I volunteered for the expedition," said Lorenzen. His face felt hot. "Isn't that enough?"

"No. So far, you're only a set of scores, multi-dimensional profiles, empirical formulas and numbers. I'd like to know you as a human being, John. I'm not trying to pry. I just want to be friends."

"All right." Lorenzen took a long drink. "Fire away."

"No questions. This isn't an analysis. Just a conversation." Avery sighed again. "Lord, I'll be glad when we get into space! You've no idea what a rat race the whole business has been, right from the first. If our friend Thornton knew all the details, he'd probably conclude it wasn't God's will that man should go to Troas. He might be right, at that. Sometimes I wonder."

"The first expedition got back—"

"That wasn't the Lagrange expedition. That was a shipful of astronomers, simply investigating the stars of the Hercules cluster. They found the Troas-Ilium system in the course of studying the Lagrange suns, and took some data from space—enough to make a planetographic survey seem worthwhile—but they didn't land."

"The first *real* Lagrange expedition never came back."

There was silence in the room. Outside the broad windows, the night city burned against darkness.

"And we," said Lorenzen finally, "are the second."

"Yes. And everything has been going wrong, I

tell you. First the Institute had to spend three years raising the money. Then there were the most fantastic mix-ups in their administration. Then they started building the ship—they couldn't just buy one, everything was committed elsewhere—and there were delays all along the line. This part wasn't available, that part had to be made special. It ran the time of building, and the cost, way over estimate. Then—this is confidential, but you might as well know it—there was sabotage. The main converter went wild on its first test. Only the fact that one man stuck by his post saved it from being a total loss. Even as it was, the repairs and the delay exhausted the Institute's treasury, and there was another pause while they raised more money. It wasn't easy; public apathy toward the whole idea of colonization is growing with each failure.

"They're almost ready now. There are still hitches—this business tonight was just a small sample—but the job is almost done." Avery shook his head. "It's fortunate that the director of the Institute, and Captain Hamilton, and a few others, have been so stubborn about it. Ordinary men would have given up years ago."

"Years . . . yes, it's about seven years since the first expedition disappeared, isn't it?" asked Lorenzen.

"Uh-huh,. Five years since the Institute started planning this one."

"Who . . . who were the saboteurs?"

"Nobody knows. Maybe some fanatic group with its own distorted motives. There are a lot of them, you know. Or maybe . . . no, that's too fantastic. I'd rather assume that Lagrange Expedition II has had a run of bad luck, and hope that the run is about over."

"And Expedition I?" asked Lorenzen softly.

"I don't know. Who does? It's one of the things we're supposed to find out."

They were quiet then for a long time. The unspoken thought ran between them: *It looks as if somebody or something doesn't want men on Troas. But who, and why, and how?*

We're supposed to find the answer. But we're also supposed to bring the answer back. And the first expedition, as well equipped and as well manned as ours, did not return.

CHAPTER III

"—INTERSTELLAR distances have become almost meaningless with invention of the warp drive—within an enormous range. It does not take appreciably more time and energy to go 100,000 light-years than to go one. As a natural result, once the nearer stars had been visited, explorers from Sol started investigating the most interesting ones in the Galaxy, even though many of these lie very far indeed from home, and temporarily ignoring the millions of intervening but quite ordinary suns. In the 22 years since the first Alpha Centauri expedition, hundreds of stars have been reached; and if the hope of finding Earth-like planets for colonization has so far been blasted, the reward in terms of scientific knowledge has been considerable.

"The first expedition to the Hercules cluster was purely astronomical, the personnel being interested only in the astrophysics of the cluster: a dense group composed of millions of stars belonging to Population II, with a surrounding space singularly clear of dust and gases. But while circling the double star Lagrange, the observers detected a planet and investigated. It turned out to be a double planet, the larger remarkably terrestroid. From its Trojan position, it was named Troas, the smaller companion named Ilium. Lacking facilities for planetfall, the expedition necessarily contented itself with studies from space . . . ''

Lorenzen put down the pamphlet with a sigh. Almost, he knew it by heart. Spectrographic data on the atmosphere, yes, and the vegetation observed seemed to hold chlorophyl. Calculations of mass and surface gravity. Thermocouples confirming what the maps showed: a world still in the clutch of glaciers, but the equatorial regions cool and bracing, a climate which knew snow and storm but also the flowering of summer. A world where men could perhaps walk unarmored, and build homes and farms and cities, a world where men could possibly grow roots and belong. The seven billion humans jammed into the Solar System were crying for a place to go. And during his lifetime he had seen the slow withering of the dream.

It had been foreseen, of course, but no one had believed it till one ship after another had come trailing home, the dust of stars on her battered hull, to bring the word. In all the Galaxy's swarming myriads of planets, there might be none where men could strike roots.

Life on Earth is such a delicate balance of chemical, physical, and ecological factors, many of them due to sheer geological and evolutionary accident, that the probability of a world where men could live without elaborate artificial aids is lower than one dares think. First you have to find an oxygen atmosphere, the proper range of radiation and temperature, a gravity not too small to let the air escape and not so great as to throw the human body fluid adjustment out of kilter. That alone winnows the worlds like some great machine; you have less than one percent left. And then you have to start on the biology of it. Vegetation nourishing to man, and the domestic animals which can eat it, cannot grow without a gigantic web of other life, most of it microscopic: nitrogen-fixing bacteria, saprophytes, earthworms—and these cannot simply be seeded on a new world, for they in turn are dependent on other life-forms. You have to give them an ecology into which they can fit. A billion years of separate evolution will most likely produce native life which is inedible or sheer poison; what, for instance, are the odds against the duplication of all the vitamins?

Mars and Venus and the Jovian moons had been colonized, yes, but it had been at enormous expense and for special reasons—mining, penal colonies, refugees during two centuries of war and tyranny. But their system of domes and tank food could never support many, however hard you tried. Now when the stars were open, nobody wanted another hell-planet. In money terms—which, ultimately, means in terms of value received for effort expended—it wouldn't pay.

A few worlds might have been colonizable. But they held diseases to which man had no racial immunity whatsoever, which would surely wipe out ninety percent of any colony before serums and vaccines could be developed. (The dying crew of the *Magellan,* returning from Sirius to radio their tragic message before they plunged their ship into the sun.) Or there were natives, unhuman beings as bright as man; often with their own technologies not too far behind his. They would resist invasion, and the logistics of interstellar conquest were merely ridiculous. Balancing the cost of sending colonists and their equipment (lives, too-scarce material resources, blood, sweat, and tears) and the cost of sending soldiers, against the probable gain (a few million humans given land, and the economics of space travel such that they could ship little of value back to Sol), yielded a figure too far in the red. Conquest was theoretically possible, but a war-exhausted humanity, most of it still living near the starvation level, wasn't that interested in empire.

Wanted: terrestroid planets, habitable but uninhabited, clean of major sicknesses, rich enough to support colonists without help from Sol.

Found: In almost a generation, nothing.

Lorenzen remembered the wave of excitement which had followed the return of the Hercules expedition. He had still been a boy then—that was the year before he got the scholarship to Rio Polytechnic—but he, too, had looked up through a wintry Alaskan night to the cold arrogance of the stars; he had also flung his head back with a laugh.

And the *Da Gama* had set out and had left Sol behind her. And after two years, men shrugged with a weariness that was dying hope. Murdered by natives or by microbes, gulped down when the earth opened under them, frozen by a sudden blast from the glacial north—who knew? Who cared? You heard little talk nowadays about New Earth; no utopian schemes for the fresh start man was going to make were being published; more and more, men put their shoulders to the tired old wheel of Earth, resigned to this being their only home and their only hope through all time forever.

"Two swallows do not make a summer . . . Statistically inadequate sample . . . Statistical certainty that *somewhere* there must be . . . " But funds for more investigations were whittled down in every session of Parliament. More and more of the great star ships swung darkly about Earth while their captains begged for finances. And when the Lagrange Institute dug into its own treasury to buy one of them, it could not be done, there was always a reason. "Sorry, but we want to keep her; as soon as we can raise the money, we want to try an idea of our own . . . Sorry, but she's already committed; leaving in two months for an xenological expedition to Tau Ceti . . . Sorry, but we're converting her to an interplanetary freighter, that's where the money is . . . Sorry." The *Henry Hudson* had to be built from scratch.

The Egyptians sailed to Punt, and could easily have gone further; with a little development, their ships could have reached the Indies. The Alexandrians built an aeolipile, but there was enough slave labor around so that they had no reason to go on from there and make a steam turbine. The Romans printed their maps, but didn't apply the idea to books. The Arabs developed algebra and then got more interested in theological hairsplitting. Something has always lain within the grasp of man which he just didn't care to take hold of. Society must want something enough for the wish to become an actual need before it gets the thing.

The starward wish was dying.

CHAPTER IV

SOL was two billion kilometers behind them, little more than the brightest star in a frosty swarm, when they went into warp. The engines roared, building up toward the potentials beyond which the omega effect set in. There was a wrenching dizziness as the ship and her crew leaped out of normal energy levels; night and confusion while the atoms readjusted in their non-Dirac matrices. Then quiet, and utter blind blackness outside the viewports.

It was like an endless falling through nullity. The ship could not accelerate, could not spin, for there was nothing which she could move in relation to; for the duration of the trip, she was *irrelevant* to the four-dimensional universe. Weight came back as the inner hull started rotating with respect to the outer, though Lorenzen had already been sick—he never could stand free fall. Then there was nothing to do but settle down for the month or so it would take to reach Lagrange.

And the days passed, swept out by clocks, unmarked by any change—they were only waiting now, doubly held in timelessness. Fifty men, spacers and scientists, fretted out the emptiness of hours and wondered what lay on the other end of the warp.

It was on the fifth day when Lorenzen and Tetsuo Hideki wandered down toward the main lounge. The Manchurian was one of the organic chemists: a small, frail-looking, soft-spoken fellow in loose robes, timed with people and highly competent in his work. Lorenzen thought that Hideki made a barrier against the world out of his test tubes and analyzers, but he rather liked the Asian. *I've done pretty much the same myself, haven't I? I get along all right with people, yes, but down underneath I'm afraid of them.*

"—but why can't you say that it takes us a month to go to Lagrange? That is the time we measure aboard ship, is it not? It is also the time a Lagrangian or Solarian observer would measure between the moment we entered the warp and the moment we came out."

"Not quite," said Lorenzen. "The math shows that it's meaningless to equate time measured inside the warp with time measured outside. It's not even similar to the time-shift in classical relativity. In the omega-effect equations, the t and t' are two distinct expressions, two different dimensions; they have about the same numerical value, but the conversion factor is not a pure number. The fact that time spent in the warp is about the same no matter how far you go—within a terrifically big

radius, up to the point where space curvature become significant—indicates that we don't have a
true velocity at all.'' He shrugged. ''I don't pre-
tend to understand the whole theory. Not a dozen
men can.''

''This is your first interstellar trip, is it not,
John?''

''Uh-huh. I've never been further than the
Moon before.''

''I have never even been off Earth. I believe
Captain Hamilton and a couple of engineers are
the only men aboard who have flown the star ways
before now. It is strange.'' Hideki's eyes looked
scared. ''There is much which is strange about this
trip. I have never heard of so ill-assorted a crew.''

''N-n-no.'' Lorenzen thought over those he
knew anything about. There had already been
clashes, which Avery had not succeeded very well
in smoothing over. ''But the Institute had to take
what it could get, I suppose, and there are all too
many lunatic opinions left over from the wars and
the Interregnum. Political fanatics, racial fanatics,
religious fanatics—'' His voice trailed off.

''I take it you support the Solar government?''

''Sure. I may not like everything it does, but it's
got to compromise with many elements if it's to be
democratic, and stamp out many others if it's to
survive. It's all that stands between us and a return
of anarchy and tyranny.''

''You are right,'' said Hideki. ''War is a monster;
my people know that.'' There was a darkness in

his eyes. Lorenzen wondered if he was thinking of the Mongku Empire which Mars had shattered, or if his thoughts went still further back, to the lovely lost islands of Japan and the Fourth World War which had sunk them under the sea.

They came to the entrance of the lounge and paused, looking in to see who was there. It was a big, low room, its furniture and drapes and gentle illumination a rest from the impersonal metallic harshness which was most of the ship; but it seemed rather bare. The Institute had not had time or money to decorate it properly. They should have taken time, thought Lorenzen. Men's nerves were worn thin out here between the stars, and they needed murals and a bar and a fireplace full of crackling logs. They needed home.

Avery and Gummus-lugil, the ship's chess fiends, were hunched over a board. Miguel Fernandez of Uruguay, geologist, a small dark lively young man, sat thrumming a guitar; near him was Joab Thornton, reading his Bible—no, it was Milton this time, and there was a curious lost ecstasy on the ascetic features. Lorenzen, who dabbled with art, thought that the Martian had a fascinating set of angles and planes in his face; he'd like to do his portrait sometime.

Gummus-lugil looked up and saw the newcomers. He was a dark, stocky man, his face broad and hook-nosed, his shirt open over a wiry pelt. "Hello, there," he said cheerfully.

"Hello," said Lorenzen. He rather liked the

Turk. Gummus-lugil had come up the hard way. It had marked him: he was rude and dogmatic and had no use for literature; but his mind was good. He and Lorenzen had already sat through several watches arguing politics and analytical philosophy and the chances of the Academy team getting the meteor polo pennant next year. "Who's ahead?"

"This bastard, I'm afraid."

Avery reached out and advanced a bishop. "Guard queen," he said. His voice remained almost apologetic.

"Huh? Oh, yes . . . yes . . . Let's see—" Gummus-lugil swore. "This is going to cost me a knight. Okay, okay." He moved.

Avery avoided the knight, but took a pawn with his rook. "Mate in . . . five moves," he said. "Care to resign?"

"Whuzzat?" Feverishly, Gummus-lugil studied the board. Fernandez' fingers rippled down a chord.

"You see, here . . . and here . . . and then—"

"Goddammit, stop that racket!" snarled Gummus-lugil. "How d'you expect me to concentrate?"

Fernandez flushed angrily. "I have as much right—"

Gummus-lugil showed his teeth. "If you could play, it'd be all right," he snapped. "But go do your caterwauling somewhere else, sonny boy."

"Hey, there, Kemal, take it easy." Avery looked alarmed.

Surprisingly, Thornton joined in on the engineer's side. "This should be a place for peace and quiet," he clipped. "Why don't you go play in your bunkroom, Señor Fernandez?"

"There are men off watch there who have to sleep," answered the Uruguayan. He stood up, knotting his fists together. "And if you think you can dictate to the rest of us—"

Lorenzen stood back, feeling the helpless embarrassment which quarrels always gave him. He tried to say something, but his tongue seemed thick in his mouth.

Friedrich von Osten chose that moment to enter. He stood in the farther doorway, swaying a little. It was well known he'd smuggled a case of whisky aboard. He wasn't an alcoholic, but there were no women along and he couldn't be polishing his beloved guns forever. A mercenary soldier in the ruins of Europe—even if he does get picked up for the Solar Academy, and makes good in the Patrol, and is named chief gunner for a star ship—doesn't develop other interests.

"Vot iss?" he asked thickly.

"None of your damn business!" flared Gummus-lugil. Their two jobs had already required them to work together a lot, and they just didn't get along. Two such arrogant souls couldn't.

"I make it my damn business, den." Von Osten stepped forward, hunching his great shoulders; the yellow beard bristled, and the wide battered face was red. "So you are picking on Miguel again?"

"I can handle my own affairs," stated Fernandez flatly. "You and this Puritan crank can stay out of them."

Thornton bit his lip. "I wouldn't talk about cranks," he said, rising to his own feet.

Fernandez got a wild look about him. Everybody knew that his family on the mother's side had spearheaded the Sebastianist Rebellion a century ago; Avery had quietly passed the word along with a warning not to mention it.

"Now, Joab—" The government man hastened toward the Martian, waving his hands in the air. "Now take it easy, gentlemen, please—"

"If all you fuse-blown gruntbrains would mind your own business—" began Gummus-lugil.

"Iss no such t'ing as own business here!" shouted von Osten. "Ve iss all *zusammen*— togedder, and I vould vish to put you under Patrol discipline—vun day only!"

Trust him to say exactly the wrong thing at the wrong moment, thought Lorenzen sickly. *His being essentially right only makes it the more insufferable*.

"Look—" He opened his mouth, and the stutter that always grabbed him when he was excited made him wordless again.

Gummus-lugil took a stiff-legged step toward the German. "If you want to step outside a minute, we'll settle that," he said.

"*Gentlemen!*" wailed Avery.

"Are they, now?" asked Thornton.

"Und du kannst auch herausgehen!" bellowed von Osten, turning on him.

"Nobody insults me," snarled Fernandez. His small wiry body gathered itself as if to attack.

"Keep out of this, sonny," said Gummus-lugil. "It's bad enough your starting it."

Fernandez made a noise that was half a sob and jumped for him. The Turk sprang back in surprise. When a fist grazed his cheek, his own leaped out and Fernandez lurched back.

Von Osten yelled and swung at Gummus-lugil. "Give me a hand," gasped Avery. "Get them apart!" He almost dragged Thornton along with him. The Martian got a grip on von Osten's waist and pulled. The German kicked at his ankles. Thornton snapped his lips together over a cry of pain and tried to trip his opponent. Gummus-lugil stood where he was, panting.

"What the devil is going on here?"

They all turned at that shout. Captain Hamilton stood in the doorway.

He was a tall man, solidly built, heavy-featured, thick gray hair above the deep-lined face. He wore the blue undress uniform of the Union Patrol, in which he was a reservist, with mathematical correctness. His normally low voice became a quarterdeck roar, and the gray eyes were like chill iron as they swept the group.

"I thought I heard a quarrel in here—but a brawl!"

They moved away from each other, sullenly,

looking at him but not meeting his gaze.

He stood for a very long while, regarding them with a raking contempt. Lorenzen tried to make himself small. But down somewhere inside himself, he wondered how much of that expression was a good job of acting. Hamilton was a bit of a martinet, yes, and he'd had himself psyched as thoroughly as he could be, to rid of all fears and compulsions irrelevant to his work—but he couldn't be that much of a machine. He had children and grandchildren in Canada; he liked gardening; he was not unsympathetic when—

"All of you here have university degrees." The captain was speaking very quietly now. "You're educated men, scientists and technicians. You're the cream of Sol's intellect, I'm told. Well, if you are, God help us all!"

There was no answer.

"I suppose you know expeditions like this are dangerous enough at best," went on Hamilton. "I also believe you were told that the first expedition to Troas never got back. To me, it seems reasonable that if we're to survive at all, we have to make a team and work together against whatever it was that killed the first ship. Apparently it does not seem so to you."

He grinned with careful nastiness. "Presumably you scientists also think I'm just the pilot. I'm just a conductor whose only business is to get you to Troas and back. If you believe that, I advise you to read the articles again—assuming you can read.

I'm responsible for the safety of the whole ship, including your lives, God help me. That means I'm the boss, too. From the moment you entered the airlock at Earth to the moment you leave it again back at Earth, I'm the boss.

"I don't give one spitball in hell who started this or who did what in which manner to whom. It's enough that there was a fight where there shouldn't have been one. You're all going in the brig for a day—without food. Maybe that'll teach you some manners."

"But I didn't—" whispered Hideki.

"Exactly," snapped Hamilton. "I want every man aboard to have a vested interest in preventing this sort of thing. If your lives, and the lives of everybody else, don't matter to you, maybe your fat-gutted bellies will."

"But I *tried* —" wailed Avery.

"And failed. A rust-eaten failure if I ever saw one. You get brigged for incompetence, Mr. Avery. It's your job to see that tensions don't build up this way. All right, now—march!"

They marched. Not a word was said.

Somewhat later, Hideki murmured in the darkness of the brig: "It isn't fair. Who does he think he is, God Almighty?"

Lorenzen shrugged, his own easy-going temperament asserting itself, "A captain has to be, I guess."

"But if he keeps this up, everyone will hate him!"

"I imagine he's a pretty good rule-of-thumb psychman himself. Quite probably that's what he wants."

Later, lying in blindness on a hard narrow bunk, Lorenzen wondered what had gone wrong. Avery talked to all the men privately, counseled them, tried to ease their fears and hatreds so that they wouldn't turn on others. At least, he was supposed to. But he hadn't. Incompetent ass! Maybe there was a curse on Lagrange after all.

CHAPTER V

THE SKY was incredible.

Here in the center of the great cluster, the double star was a double blaze. Lagrange I seemed as bright as Sol, though only half the apparent size, a blue-green flame ringed with eerie halos of corona and zodiacal light. When the glare was filtered out, you could see monstrous prominences on its rim. Lagrange II, a third of Sol's angular diameter but almost as luminous, was a rich orange-red, like a huge coal flung into heaven. When both their lights streamed through the viewports into a darkened room, men's faces had an unearthly color; they seemed themselves transfigured.

The stars were so brilliant that some of them could be seen even through that haze of radiance. When you looked out from the shadow side of the ship, the sky was a hard crystal black spattered with stars—great unwinking diamonds, flashing and flashing, confused myriads, a throng of them glittering in a glory such as Earth's dwellers had never seen. It was lonely to think that their light, which Earth now saw, had left when man was still huddled in caves; that the light now streaming from them would be seen in an unthinkable future when there might be no more men on Earth.

The *Hudson* had taken an orbit about Troas, some 4,000 kilometers out. The companion, Ilium, looked almost four times as big as Luna seen from Earth; the limb was blurred by the thin atmosphere, and the harsh glare of dead seabottoms mottled the bluish face. A small world, old before its time, no place to colonize; but it would be a rich near-by source of minerals for men on Troas.

That planet hung enormous in the viewports, filling nearly half the sky. You could see the air about it, clouds and storms, day and night. The ice-caps covering a third of its face were blinding white, the restless wind-whipped oceans were a blueness which focused the light of one sun to a cruel point. There were islands and one major continent, its north and south ends buried under the ice, spreading easterly and westerly halfway round the planet. It was green about the equator, hazing into darker green and brown toward the poles. Lakes and rivers were like silver threads across it. A high mountain range, rugged sweep of light and shadow, ran down either coast.

The half-dozen men in the ship's observatory hung in weightless silence. The mingled light of the suns gleamed off the metal of their instruments. They were supposed to compare notes on their several observations, but for a while they didn't want to speak; this was too awesome.

"Well?" Hamilton barked it out at last. "What have you found?"

"Essentially—" Lorenzen gulped. The anti-space sickness pills helped some, but he still felt weak, he longed for weight and clean air. "Essentially, we've confirmed what the Hercules expedition noted. Mass of the planets, distance, atmosphere, temperature—and yes, the green down there definitely has the absorption spectrum of chlorophyl."

"Any sign of life?"

"Oh, yes, quite a bit of it. Not only the plants, but animals, huge herds of them. I've got plenty of photographs." Lorenzen shook his head. "Not a trace of the *Da Gama,* though. We've looked for two of the planet's days, and we could surely have spotted their boats or an abandoned camp. But nothing."

"Could they have landed on Sister and come to grief there?" Christopher Umfanduma, the African biologist, gestured at the stark face of Ilium.

"No," said Hamilton. "Doctrine for these survey trips is that the expedition goes first to the planet it was announced it will go to. If for any reason they then go elsewhere, they leave a cairn big enough to be seen from space. We can check Sister, but my conviction is that the trouble happened on Junior. Sister is too typical, it's like Mars; nothing much *can* happen to well-trained spacemen on a place like that."

"Other planets in this system?" asked Hideki. "Maybe they—"

"No, there aren't any. Just a stinking little

group of asteroids in the other Trojan position. Planetary formation theory and considerations of stability just about prohibit anything else. You know, don't you, that Junior doesn't have true Trojan stability? No planet of a double star can have it; the mass ratio of the suns is always too small. Junior is only metastable because of Sister's effect. Not that it makes any difference on the time scale of human history. No, there are no other planets here."

"Of course," ventured Avery, very softly, "the expedition could perhaps have left Troas in good form and perished on the way home."

Hamilton snorted. "Nothing can happen to a ship in the warp. No, it's down—" his deep-set eyes went to the plane and rested there, darkly— "it's down on Junior that whatever happened to them, happened. But why no trace of them? The *Da Gama* herself ought still to be in orbit up here. The boats ought to be visible down there. Were they sunk into the ocean?"

"By whom?" Avery said it into a sudden enormous quiet. "Or by what?"

"There's no trace of intelligent life, I tell you," said Lorenzen wearily. "At this distance, our telescopes could spot anything from a city or an aircraft to the thatch hut of some savage."

"Maybe they don't build huts," said Avery. His face looked abstracted.

"Shut up," snapped Hamilton. "You've got no business here anyway. This is a mapping room."

Hideki shivered. "It looks cold down there," he said. "Bleak."

"It isn't," said Fernandez. "Around the equator, the climate ought to be rather like, say, Norway or Maine. And you will note that the trees and grasses go right up to the swamps at the foot of the glaciers. Glacial periods aren't anywhere near as barren as people think; Earth was full of animal life in the Pleistocene, and it wasn't till hunting got worse when the glaciers receded that man was forced to develop agriculture and become civilized. Anyway, those glaciers are on the way out; I've seen distinct moraines in the photographs. When we settle here and jack up the carbon dioxide content of the air, you will be surprised how fast Junior will develop its own tropics. A few hundred years, perhaps. Geologically, nothing!" He snapped his fingers and grinned.

"*If* we settle it," grunted Hamilton. "Now, how long before you can have reliable maps, Lorenzen?"

"Uummm—well—a week, maybe. But do we have to wait that long?"

"We do. I want one overall map on a scale of one to a million, and enough others to cover the central valley region where we'll land—say from five degrees on either side of the equator —on one to 10,000. Print up about fifty copies of each. Run your prime meridian through the north magnetic pole; you can send down a roboflyer to locate it."

Lorenzen groaned inwardly. He had the cartographic machines to help him, but it wasn't going to be fun.

"I'll take a boat and a few men and run over for a closer look at Sister," went on Hamilton. "Not that I expect to find anything much, but—" Suddenly he grinned. "You can name the conspicuous features down there anything you like, but for God's sake don't be like that Chilean map-man at Epsilon Eridani III! His maps had been official for ten years before they found out every one of his names was an Araucanian obscenity!"

He clapped the astronomer's shoulder and pulled himself out of the room. *Not a bad sort,* thought Lorenzen. *He's a better psychman than Avery; though Ed isn't such a slouch either. He just lacks personality.*

He decided to stick by the classical nomenclature of the Hercules expedition. Mount Olympus, Mount Ida, the huge river down there would be the Scamander—and, of course, it wouldn't last. When the colonists came, it would be Old Baldy, Conchinjangua, Novaya Neva—

If the colonists came.

"Let's, uh, let's get organized," he said aloud, awkwardly. "How many here know anything about cartography?"

"I do," said Avery unexpectedly. "I'll help out if you wish."

"Where in cosmos did you pick that up?" asked Fernandez.

"Part of my education. A lot of applied

psychodynamics consists of conformal mapping, though we generally have to use spaces of several dimensions and and non-Cartesian coordinates. I can handle a mapping machine as well as you can."

Lorenzen blinked. After a moment, he nodded. The modern science of human behavior was out of his line, but he'd seen some of the texts: They used more paramathematical symbols than his own.

He crooked an arm around a hand rung and let his legs stream out behind him. Avery had said his tendency to space sickness was mostly psychological. It might help him to take his mind off the work and the coldly shining planet out there, just for a few minutes.

"How precise is your science, anyway?" he asked. "The popular articles on it are always so vague."

"Well—" Avery rubbed his chin. He hung cross-legged in the air like a small Buddha, his eyes remote. "Well, we don't claim the precision of the physical sciences," he said finally. "In fact, it's been shown rigorously that we can never achieve it: a kind of uncertainty principle of our own, due to coupling between observer and system observed. But a lot has been learned."

"Such as what?" inquired Umfanduma. "I know about the advances in neurology; that's in my own line. But how about man as—as man, instead of as a biophysical mechanism?"

"The amount of knowledge depends on the particular field of study," said Avery. "Already before World War III, they were using games theory in military work, and later the big computers made it possible to analyze even complex phenomena like business from a theoretical viewpoint; that in turn led to some understanding of economics. Communications theory turned out to be widely applicable: man is, after all, essentially a symbolizing animal. The least effort axiom was useful. Gradually a mathematical and paramathematical system has been built up, in which the elements—potentials, gradients, and so on—can be equated with observable phenomena; thus it becomes possible to derive theorems. It's still hard to check the validity of many of these theorems because conditions at home are too confused even today and, of course, you can't very well run a controlled experiment with human beings; but insofar as we have data, they confirm the present theories. Quite often it's possible to predict large-scale things like economic cycles with high precision."

"Didn't the dictators know most of that?" asked Lorenzen. "They certainly had effective propaganda techniques. I was more interested in modern developments."

"Most of it is modern," snorted Avery. "Very little that went before was of scientific value. To consider only the history of my own region, North America: The propagandists of capital and labor, the advertising men, worked on such a primitive level, with such a primitive appeal, that quite often they produced a reaction against themselves. They were only part of the mass-psychological debacle that led to military defeat. The commissars were mentally blinkered by their own outworn ideology; they never dared investigate beyond its dogma. The self-styled liberators were only interested in getting that power for themselves; it wasn't their propaganda which won the people to them, but the commissars' tyranny, and they were soon just as unpopular. The warlords during the Interregnum did have psychomilitary analysts, yes, but the only original work then was done in Brazil. Later, in the theocratic period, research was pushed because the Mongku Empire presented a challenge, and the first politicomathematical analyses were performed. But it wasn't till after Venus had taken over and Earth was temporarily at peace and the theocrats tossed out of America, that really thorough research was done. Then, of course, we finally got the formulated psychodynamics, the field and tensor approach, and it was used to bring on the Mars-Venus war and unify the Solar System—but the completed science had been worked out by peaceful professors interested only in the problem itself; their type is still doing all the major new work."

"Whew!" laughed Umfanduma.

"Completed science, did you say?" inquired Lorenzen. "I thought—"

"Oh, yes, work is still going on, all the time. But

the results are already far enough along to be of inestimable value. Control of the economic cycle, for instance; the most efficient distribution of cities; currency stabilization; the gradual weaning of man away from barbarism toward the first really mature civilization —a civilization where *everyone* is sane.'' Something glowed behind the pudgy face and the blinking pale eyes. ''It's a heartbreakingly big job, it'll take centuries and there'll be many setbacks and failures and mistakes—but at least, for the first time in history, we have not only good intentions, but some idea of how to implement them.''

''Yes, I suppose so,'' murmured Lorenzen. His mind continued: *You can't elect a psychocrat, any more than you can elect an engineer. I don't want an elite of any kind, the world has seen too many of them; with all its maddening drawbacks, par- liamentary government is still the only way; the psychocrats must still remain only advisors.*

But one gets into the habit of letting the advisors lead–

He sighed and shoved away from the wall. ''Come on,'' he said. ''Work to do.''

CHAPTER VI

LORENZEN KNEW that an unknown planet was approached cautiously, but the knowledge had only been in the top of his head. This was the first time he lived through that care, and it nearly drove him crazy.

When the maps were ready, four boats descended—forty men, with a skeleton crew remaining on the *Hudson* in her orbit. Fernandez sweated on the way down; it was he who had picked the landing site, and his fault if it turned out to be a morass or an earthquake region. But nothing happened.

That was exactly the trouble—nothing happened. They landed some kilometers from the Scamander, on a wide green plain dotted with clumps of trees and hazing into blue distance. Silence fell when the rockets were cut off; the grass fire they had started burned itself out; and men stared wistfully through the viewports at the sunlit world ouside.

The chemists and biologists were busy. There was detailed analysis to do—of air, of soil and vegetation samples brought in by robots.

Thornton checked radiation and reported nothing harmful. A cageful of rhesus monkeys was set outside and left for a week. During that week, nobody stirred from the boats. The robots which came and went were sterilized with savage thoroughness in the airlocks. There was nothing for the rest of the men to do.

Lorenzen buried himself in his microbooks, but even Shakespeare and Jensen and *The Song of the Jovian Men* got wearisome. Others puttered about, quibbled with each other, yawned and slept and woke blearily to another day of nothing. There were no open quarrels on this boat because Hamilton was aboard it; but the captain often had to snap furiously over the telescreen at men in the other craft.

Fernandez came close to losing his temper once. He protested to Hamilton: "You can't be that frightened of sickness!"

"I sure as hell can," grunted the captain. "If evolution on this planet is as close to Earth's as it seems to be, you can bet your degree there are some microbes which can live off us. And I want to go home on my feet. The least I can do is make reasonably sure we won't catch anything airborne."

Hideki and his team reported on such plants as they had analyzed: essentially terrestroid, though denser and tougher. Some were poisonous because of heavy-metal content or the like, but most could be eaten quite safely. A man could live well on the wild vegetation alone. It would take more study, though, to determine just how many sorts you had to eat for a balanced diet.

It was quite an event when they had their first meal of Troan food. The flavors were indescribable. Lorenzen grew aware of how impoverished most human languages are with respect to taste and smell sensations—but there were hints of ginger and cinnamon and garlic. He grinned and suggested: "Perhaps the soul of Escoffier isn't in Paradise at all; maybe he was given special permission to fly around the Galaxy and see what he could whomp up."

Thornton frowned, and Lorenzen flushed—but how do you apologize for a joke? He said nothing, but winced when he remembered the incident.

Hamilton only permitted half the men to eat that meal, and observed them closely during the day that followed.

Now and then animals were seen, most of them small fleeting shapes that scuttled through the long grasses on the edge of the burned area; but once a herd of bigger quadrupeds, the size of ponies, wandered past: grayish-green, scaled, with long hoofed legs and earless reptilian heads. Umfanduma cursed with his impatience to get a closer look.

"If the reptiles have developed that far," he said, "I'll give odds there are no mammals."

"Reptiles in a glacial period?" asked Fernandez skeptically. "Not that big, my friend."

"Oh, not reptiles strictly speaking, but closer to that stage than terrestrial mammals. There are cold and warm seasons here, I'm told, so they must have warm blood and well-developed hearts; but they certainly don't look placental."

"That's another argument in favor of there being no intelligent life here," said Lorenzen. "It looks as if this planet is wide open, just waiting for man."

"Yes . . . just waiting." Avery spoke with a sudden surprising bitterness. "Waiting for mines and cities and roads, for the hills to be leveled and the plains filled up with people. For our dogs and cats and cows and pigs to wipe out the infinite variety of native life. For noise and dust and crowding."

"Don't you like the human race, Ed?" asked Gumus-lugil sardonically. "I thought your job required you to."

"I like the human race in its proper place . . . which is Earth," said Avery. "Oh, well," He shrugged and smiled. "Never mind."

"We've got a piece of work to do," said Hamilton. "It's not our department to worry about the consequences."

"A lot of men have said that throughout history," replied the psychman. "Soldiers, executioners, scientists building atomic bombs. Well—" He turned away, sighing.

Lorenzen grimaced. He remembered the green rustling stillness of the Alaskan woods, the stark wild glory of the Lunar peaks. There was little enough of that left in the Solar System, few enough places where you could be alone. It did seem a pity that Troas—

After a week, the monkeys were brought in. Umfanduma checked them carefully, killed and dissected them, ran analyses with the help of Hideki. "All normal," he reported. "I found some types of native bacteria in their bloodstream, living harmlessly and completely sterile; apparently they can't reproduce in the chemical conditions of the terrestrial body. You wouldn't even get a fever from them."

Hamilton's lean gray head nodded. "All right," he said at last, slowly. "I guess we can go out."

He led the way. There was a brief ceremony of planting the flag of the Solar Union. Lorenzen stood bareheaded with the rest, the wind ruffling his hair under an alien sky, and thought that in this big lonely landscape the whole affair was a little ridiculous.

For a couple of days the site boiled with activity as camp was set up, men and robots working around the clock. There was always light, from the green or red sun or both, or from the great shield of Sister, high in a sky that burned with an unbelievable glory of stars. The work was hampered by friction between men, though it seemed strange that they should quarrel when they were as isolated as men had ever been. But it went on. A neat circle of collapsible shelters grew up around the clustered boats; the main generator began to throb and there was electric light; a well was tapped, a sterilizing unit built, and there was running water; a ring of detectors and alarms and guns was drawn about the camp. The shelters became sleeping quarters, a mess hall, a sick bay, several laboratories, a machine shop. Their metal half-cylinders looked harsh and out of place in the soft landscape.

After that, Lorenzen found himself rather a fifth wheel. There wasn't much for an astronomer to do. He set up a telescope, but between the suns and the satellite there was always too much light for effective study. In the scurrying busyness of the camp, he began to feel homesick.

He went in their one aircar with some others to the Scamander, to take a closer look and gather specimens. The river was enormous, a slowly rolling brown sheet; when you stood on one reedy bank, you couldn't see the other. The fish, insects, and plants didn't interest him much; as a zoological layman, he was more for the larger animals, paraphylon and astymax and tetrapterus. Hunting was easy; none of them seemed to have known anything like man and a rifle bowled them over as they approached curiously closer. Everybody wore a sidearm, for there were carnivores, you could hear them howling at night—but there was really nothing to fear from them.

There were no tall trees; the low scrubby growths which dotted the plains were incredibly tough; an ax would hardly dent them and you needed an AH torch to cut them down. The biological team reported them—on the basis of dendrochronology—to be some centuries old. They wouldn't be of much use to man; he'd have to bring his own seedlings and use forced-growth techniques if he wanted lumber. But the catalogue of edible plants and animals grew apace. A man could be set down here naked and alone, and if he knew anything at all about flint-working he could soon be comfortable.

Then what had happened to the men of the *Da Gama*?

It could not have been Junior's own environment. It wasn't that alien; as far as wild beasts and disease went, it looked safer than some parts of Earth even today. Now in the warm season, the days were bright and the rains were merely cool; there would be snow in winter, but nothing that fire and furs couldn't stave off. The low carbon dioxide content of the air required a slight change in breathing habits, but it was easily, almost unconsciously made. The lighting was weird—sometimes greenish, sometimes reddish, sometimes a blend of both, with double shadows and the colors of the landscape shifting with the suns—but it was not unpleasing, surely nothing to cause madness. There were poisonous plants, a couple of men got a bad rash from merely brushing one herb, but anyone with half a brain could soon learn to avoid those types. The land was quiet, speaking only with a sough of wind and rush of rain and thunder, remote cry of animals and beat of wings in the sky—but that too was only a relief after the clangor of civilization.

Well—

Lorenzen puttered with his instruments, measuring the exact periods of revolution and rotation for the planet and the heavenly bodies. The rest of the time he helped out, awkwardly, where he could, or talked to men off duty, or played games, or sat around and read. It wasn't his fault, this idleness, but he felt obscurely guilty about it. Maybe he should consult Avery. The psychman seemed rather a lost soul himself.

Twelve of Junior's thirty-six-hour days slipped past. And then the aliens came.

CHAPTER VII

A TELESCOPE swinging on its clockwork mounting. Sudden shapes moving in its field. A photocell reacts, and the feedback circuit holds the 'scope leveled on the approaching objects. As they come nearer, an alarm is tripped and a siren skirls into the quiet air.

Friedrich von Osten jumped from the cot on which he had been dozing. *"Lieber Gott!"* He grabbed a rifle, and loosened the magnum pistol at his waist as he ran from the tent. Other men were sticking their heads out of the shelters, looking up from their work, hurrying to their posts at the machine gun emplacements.

Von Osten reached the command post and poised on the edge of its trench, raising his field glasses. There were . . . yes . . . eight of them, walking steadily toward the camp. It was too far yet to see details, but sunlight flashed hard off metal.

He picked up the intercom mike and said harshly: "Stand by all defense stations, Iss Captain Hamilton dere?"

"Speaking. I'm up in the bow of Boat One. They

look like . . . intelligence . . . don't they?"

"*Ja,* I t'ink dey are."

"All right. Stand by. Keep them covered, but don't shoot till I say so. That's an order. No matter what happens, don't shoot till I tell you to."

"Even if dey open up on us?"

"Yes."

The siren rose to a new note. Alarm stations! General alert!

Lorenzen ran for the shack assigned to him. The camp was a scurrying confusion, shouts and thud of feet, dust swirling up to dull the drawn guns. The aircar shot overhead, rising for a bird's-eye look. *Or tetrapterus eye?* thought Lorenzen wildly. *There are no birds here. This isn't our world.*

He entered the shelter. It was crowded with a dozen men, untrained in militechnics and assigned here mostly to keep them out of the way. Avery's round face gaped at him; the light of Lagrange I, streaming in the window, looked ghastly on his skin. "Natives?" he asked.

"I . . . suppose so." Lorenzen bit his lip. "Seems to be half a dozen or so, coming on foot. What the hell are we s-s-scared of?"

Thornton's long gaunt face thrust out of a shadowed corner. "There is no point in taking chances," he said. "No telling what those . . . things . . . intend, or what powers they command. 'Be ye therefore wise as serpents—' "

" '—and harmless as doves,' " finished Avery.

"But are we?" He shook his head. "Man is still adolescent. And this reaction is . . . childish. Fear of the unknown. With all the energies we have to use, we're still afraid. It's wrong."

"The *Da Gama*," said Thornton tightly, "did not come back."

"I don't think . . . simple planet-bound natives, without so much as a city, could have been . . . responsible," said Avery.

"*Something* was," said Lorenzen. He felt cold. "They might have weapons—b-b-bacteriological—"

"It's childish, I tell you, this fear." Avery's voice wobbled. "We've all got to die sometime. We should greet them openly and—"

"And talk to them, I suppose?" Thornton grinned. "How good is your Lagrangian, Avery?"

There was silence. The noise outside had died away, now the whole camp lay waiting.

Lorenzen looked at the chronom on his wrist. It swept out the minutes, one, two, three, ten, thirty, and time was hideously stretched. It was hot in the cabin, hot and dusty. He felt sweat trickle down under his clothes.

Forever went by in an hour. And then the siren blew. *All clear . . . come out . . . but stay alert.*

Lorenzen almost bolted from the shelter. He was close enough to the point where the aliens were to get there ahead of the crowd.

A semicircle of men, rifles in the crook of their arms, faced the strangers and held back the approaching humans. Hamilton stood in front of the guard, stiff and massive, watching the newcomers out of expressionless eyes. They looked back at him, and there was no reading their faces.

Lorenzen took them in at one gulping glance, and then went back for details. He had seen films of extraterrestrials before, and these were not as unearthly as some that had already been found— but still, it was a shock to see them here in the flesh. It was the first time he truly, fully realized that man was not unique, not anything special in the immensity of creation.

They stood on their hind legs like men, though with a forward slant which reduced their potential one and three-fourths meter height by a good ten centimeters; a heavy kangaroo-like tail balanced the body, and was probably a wicked weapon for infighting. The arms were rather skinny, otherwise humanoid, but the hands had three fingers and two opposed thumbs; each finger had an extra joint, and ended in sharp blue nails. The heads were round, with tufted ears, flat black noses, pointed chins, whiskers above the wide black-lipped mouths and the long golden eyes. They seemed to be mammals—at least, they were covered with smooth gray fur, barred in darker color that formed a mask about the eyes. Their sex was probably male, though Lorenzen couldn't be sure because they were clothed: loose blouses and baggy pants apparently woven of vegetable fiber, and a kind of mukluk on the feet. They all had leather belts supporting a couple of pouches, a knife or hatchet, and what was presumably a powder horn; on their backs were small packsacks, in their hands long-barreled affairs which he took to be muzzle-loading smoothbores.

In the first moment, they all looked alike to him; then he forced himself to locate individual differences of size, build, face: they varied as much as humans.

One of them spoke, a throaty purr. When his mouth was open, you could see the long blue canine teeth, though otherwise they seemed dentally as unspecialized as man's.

Hamilton turned around. "They don't act like a war party," he said. His voice and the low murmur of wind were the only sounds. "But you can't ever tell—Avery, you're a linguist. Can you make anything out of their talk?"

"Not . . . yet." The psychman's face was shiny with sweat, and his voice jittered. Lorenzen wondered why he should be that excited. "They do have distinct words."

"Hell," grunted Gummus-lugil, "I can't even hear that. It all sounds alike to me."

Another of the strangers spoke. Straining, Lorenzen could make out the pauses between phoneme groups. He'd taken a course in comparative linguistics at college, but it was vague in his mind now.

"They act like—well, I don't know what," said Hamilton. "Except that we're obviously not great gods from the sky to them."

"Wouldn't expect that." Avery shook his head. "If they've progressed as far as gunpowder hand weapons, I imagine their society is pretty sophisticated. Those muskets look better than what they had on Earth in Newton's time."

"But where are they *from*?" cried Fernandez. "There are no cities, no roads, not even so much as a village—I doubt if there is a house in this planet!"

Hamilton shrugged. "That's what I hope we can find out." His voice grew crisp: "Avery, you work on their language, that's your line. Von Osten, maintain guards at the defense posts, and detail a man to accompany each of these creatures wherever he goes within the bounds of the camp. But no rough stuff unless they try something extremely suspicious, and no holding them here if they want to leave. The rest of you carry on as before, but keep your arms ready all the time and don't leave camp without checking with me first."

It was sensible, thought Lorenzen. The strangers didn't look formidable, but you never knew, you never knew.

Slowly, the group broke up. The aliens followed Avery docilely enough, and one by one the others quit staring after them. Lorenzen heard Fernandez' murmur: "Natives after all! And pretty highly developed, too."

"Yeh." There was an odd sag to Gummis-lugil's heavy shoulders. "It looks like this pretty well kills the idea of colonizing.''

*Which may be the death-blow to all man's
dreams about the stars.*

Lorenzen tagged along after Avery. "Can I help
you, Ed?" he asked. "I'm at loose ends, you
know.''

"You're not a linguist, John," said the
psychman. "I'm afraid you'd only be in the way."

Lorenzen felt a stinging sense of rebuff. He
gulped and persisted: "You'll need help. Somebody to act out the verbs, and—''

Avery considered for what seemed a curiously
long time. "All right," he said at last. "To start
with, anyway.''

CHAPTER VIII

THE ALIENS were offered a bunkhouse and moved into it with alacrity; another was set up for the displaced humans. They were shown through the camp and the boats, but there was no telling what they thought about it. Men noticed that they always had somebody on watch while they slept. They didn't seem to like messing with the humans, and used their own utensils to cook native food given them. But they stayed around for days, and worked hard with Avery and Lorenzen.

It seemed they called themselves Rorvan, as nearly as a human throat could form the word, Individual names emerged for them: Silish, Yanvusarran, Alasvu. Pointing to objects and acting out verbs began to give an elementary vocabulary and the whole stock of phonemes: it was a flexible tongue, they had almost fifty. Tonal qualities seemed to be important, but in analyzing his data Avery said the language was not analogous to Chinese. "I'm pretty sure it's inflected," he declared, "but I can't make head or tail out of the grammar. Possibly the tones form the inflections, but—" He sighed.

"Why not teach them English or Spanish?" inquired Lorenzen.

"I don't want to scare them off by the prospect of so much hard work. They may be just a group of wanderers who chanced on us and will decide any moment to take off again. Don't forget, they could be anything from official ambassadors to hobos or bandits, or something for which we have no word. We know nothing about the structure of their society or about them personally." Avery ran a hand through his thin hair and looked at the notes he had. "Damn it, their language just doesn't make sense!"

"Let me study your data for a while," offered Lorenzen. I know a little something about gloss-analysis."

"Not just yet, John. I want to go over it myself a few more times. I'll run off a copy for you soon."

The next day Lorenzen was asked to go in the aircar to help in a specimen-collecting expedition. He could not very well refuse, though he fumed at the delay. When he came back, Avery gave him a sheaf of papers and a wry grin.

"Here you are," he said. "I got a lot of information yesterday while you were off, but it leaves me in a worse mess than before. A lot of it contradicts what I thought I knew."

Lorenzen spent hours over the copy and had to confess himself beaten. The word for too many important things, or the meaning of a given sound, varied without discoverable rhyme or reason. Sister, for instance, was referred to as Ortu, Omanyi, Valakesh, Arbvu-djangiz, Zulei, and a whistling noise answering to nothing in any human tongue; and it looked as if each of these words took on an entirely different meaning in other sentences. It didn't seem merely a question of synonymy: you wouldn't expect the Rorvan to be so stupid as to confuse the issue thus. The name seemed to depend on the context in some obscure manner. The whole mass of conversation held nothing identifiable as a statement.

He gave up, realizing with discouragement that he was doubtless only underfoot. Avery continued working doggedly, sitting up late to ponder each day's material. But he was the only one who didn't feel a darkness of futility.

"What the devil are we staying here for, anyway?" demanded Gummus-lugil. "There are natives. They seem to be in a position to make colonization impossible. Why not just go home and get drunk and forget the whole mucking place?"

"We're supposed to complete the survey," said Lorenzen mildly.

Gummus-lugil took out a foul old pipe and began to stuff it. His heavy dark face twisted into a scowl. "Survey my rear end! You know as well as I do this is a practical expedition. We're wasting time we ought to be using to find a planet we can have."

Lorenzen sighed. "I wonder if we ever will. It was tough enough to finance this trip. D'you think anybody can raise the cash for another? There's too much to do right at home for Parliament to spend more of the public funds on what's beginning to look like a wild goose chase, and individuals with money to donate are getting few and far between.''

"Don't you care?" asked the Turk.

"Oh . . . yes. I suppose so. But I never intended to leave Sol permanently.'' With sudden understanding: ''This means a lot to you, 'though, doesn't it, Kemal?''

The engineer nodded. ''It does. It did. I'm getting to an age where I want to settle down somewhere and raise a family. Only what can a man do in the System? Work for somebody else, all his life. I want to be my own boss. I thought—oh, hell.'' His voice trailed off and he stared emptily across the plain.

"There is a bit of hope yet,'' said Lorenzen. ''It may be that the natives live underground or some such thing. That they won't care if we colonize the surface. They'd stand to benefit, even, if that's the case—trade and so on.''

"It could be.'' There was a brief flicker in Gummus-lugil's eyes, and then a hardness grew in him. One hairy hand doubled into a fist. ''But *something* happened to the first expedition! I suspect the natives murdered them and buried the traces—''

"I doubt it,'' said Lorenzen, though a thin little fear rose in his breast. ''How'd they have gotten at the ship in her orbit? How'd the personnel get so careless as to let it happen at all? No, I still think space got them somehow. A chance meteor, just at the wrong moment, or—"

"Things like that don't happen to spaceships any more."

"They could, if all the improbabilities worked out just right. Or look—you say there was an attempt to sabotage the *Hudson*?"

"Yeh. Wait a minute—d'you mean—"

"I don't mean anything, Kemal. But there are groups at home which are opposed to the whole colony idea. The Resurrectionists think it's against the will of God. The Monarchists, the Collectivists, and the Eugenicists are all fanatics and all know that even their infinitesimal chance of getting into power will be gone if men start moving out of the System. Then there's Hilton's group, with its vague fear of the whole notion, pseudoscientific ideas about extraterrestrial diseases or invasion or the colonists mutating into something different and hostile—you see?"

"A bomb planted in the *Da Gama*." Gummus-lugil rubbed his chin. "It wouldn't have been so hard; she wasn't built from the keel up like ours . . . Of course, it's hard to see how our converter could have been monkeyed with. All our workers, right down to the last electrician, were screened by the government with just that sabotage idea in mind. But it could be. It could be."

"In that case—" A small exultance rose in

Lorenzen. ''In that case, we have nothing to fear.''

''But those bastards have plenty to fear from me!'' The Turk's hand dropped to his gun.

Another day went by. The blue-green sun rose, mists swirled and dew flashed and then the grasses lay with a metallic sheen. Six hours later the red sun followed, and full day blazed. Clouds were tinted red or green, the double shadows had their color, the vegetation shimmered in shifting hues as wind ruffled it. The first sunset was not so spectacular, with Lagrange II still high in the sky, but the late afternoon had an eerie quality when the only light was its fiery glow. Paradox: it grew cool, even a little chilly, when only the smaller sun was up, but the unearthly red radiance suggested a furnace. The second sunset was usually a gorgeous bursting of crimson and orange and gold. Then it was night, with a glittering glory of stars. Sister came up, red on one limb and blue-green on the other, the center a dimness of shadow vaguely lit by reflection from Junior. On the horizon, she looked enormous, seeming to fill half the sky; when well up, she was still so big that men used to Luna could not get rid of an uneasy notion that she was falling on them. Her light was a weird white rush of argence, glimmering off dew and hoarfrost. The night was big and still and strange to man.

It caught at Lorenzen. He walked alone in the chill quiet, thinking his own thoughts, and felt the challenge of the sky and the world about him.

Maybe he would want to come here after all. A new planet would be wide open for any man; he could have his own observatory on a space station, try out his own ideas, look at his own land and realize it was his and his children's.

But the natives—His spirits sagged again.

Another day and another.

Lorenzen was sitting under his usual tree with his usual book when he heard his name called. He looked up, and the camp's loudspeaker rolled and boomed with Hamilton's voice: "—report to the captain's office." He got up, wondering, and made his way back inside the circle of guns.

Hamilton sat at a desk in one of the huts. Avery stood beside him, looking nervous. Thornton, Fernandez, Gummus-lugil, and von Osten were already there, waiting.

"All here," said the captain quietly. "You may pass on your report, Mr. Avery."

The psychman cleared his throat. "I've made a little headway with the Rorvan language," he said. He spoke so low that it was hard to hear him. "Not much—I still don't understand the grammar or whatever it is they have, and any ideas above an elementary level just don't get across. But we can talk about very simple things. Today they said they want to go home. I couldn't follow their reason, though I imagine they want to report their findings."

"All of them going?" asked Thornton.

"Yes. I offered to have them flown home, but

they refused. Why, I don't know. They couldn't have misunderstood me, I *think*. I took them to the aircar and made gestures. But maybe they don't trust us that much. They insist on going on foot."

"Where is their home?" inquired Lorenzen.

"Somewhere to the west, in the mountains. That's all I was able to gather. About a four-week hike, I'd say."

"Vell?" snapped von Osten. "Vot iss vit' us to do?"

"The Rorvan," said Avery slowly, "were quite unhappy at the thought of our following them by air. I don't know why—it could be a taboo of some sort, or more probably they just don't trust us not to throw bombs down on their home. We're as much an unknown quantity to them as they to us, remember. If we tried to follow, I rather imagine they'd just disappear in the mountains and we might never re-establish contact. However—" he leaned forward—"there didn't seem to be any objection to some of us accompanying them on foot. In fact, they seemed anxious that we do so."

"Valking right into a trap? *Ich danke!*" Von Osten shook his head till the blond beard swirled.

"Don't be more of an ass than you can help," said Gummus-lugil. "They'd know the rest of our party could take revenge."

"Could dey now?" Von Osten flushed and held himself in check with an effort. "How vould de oders know vere ve vere?"

"Radio, of course," said Hamilton impatiently.

"You'd take a portable transceiver along—"

"But do de aliens know ve haff radio?"

"That's a good point," admitted the captain. "The chances are they've never heard of the phenomenon. And I don't think they should be told about it either—not till we can trust them more."

He made a bridge of his fingers. "Mr. Avery wants to go along with them, and I agree that we should send some men. It may well be our only chance to get in touch with the native government, or whatever it is they have. To say nothing of getting a closer look at their technology and all the rest of it. After all, they may not object to humans coming here to settle. We just don't know yet, and it's our job to find out.

"You gentlemen here aren't needed for the studies we're making, your essential work has been done and you seem logical choices for the contact party. You'll keep in touch with the camp by radio and, of course, make observations as you go along. I won't hide the possible dangers from you. There may be diseases, poisonous snakes, or anything else you can imagine. The Rorvan, not knowing that I'll know exactly where you are, may indeed murder you. But all in all, I think it's fairly safe for you to go. It's strictly volunteer, of course, and no shame to the man who doesn't wish to stick his neck out—but are you willing?"

Lorenzen wasn't sure. He admitted to himself he was frightened, just a little, and would rather stay in camp. But what the hell—everybody else was agreeing. "Sure," he said.

Afterward it occurred to him that the fear of being the only hold-back might have prompted all the others too. Man was a funny animal.

CHAPTER IX

THE FIRST three or four days were pure anguish.
Then muscles got used to it, and they were logging
off some forty kilometers a day without undue
strain. It got monotonous, just walking over a
prairie that always receded into far distances. Rain
didn't stop them, the humans slipped on their
waterproof coveralls and the Rorvan didn't seem
to mind. There were broad rivers, but all of them
shallow enough to ford, and canteens could be
filled there. The long-range terrestrial rifles
knocked down the plentiful game at distances of a
kilometer or two, and on days when no animals
appeared there was always plenty of wild vegetation, stems and leaves and beans which were
nourishing if tough. Gummus-lugil, who carried
the transceiver, signalled back to camp every
evening—a dot-dash system, to keep the Rorvan
from suspecting what the radio was. Hamilton had
established three triangulation robostations which
kept him informed of the party's whereabouts. His
own reports held nothing exciting, merely further
details on what they already knew.

The Rorvan used compasses and maps to guide

them, the latter in a symbology easy enough to translate once you knew what the various features were; they were hand-drawn, though that didn't mean the aliens didn't know about printing, and had a delicate touch —almost Chinese. The Mercator projection with its grid of lines and what was probably the prime meridian going straight through the south magnetic pole, suggested that they knew the true shape of the planet.

Lorenzen grew aware of the personality differences between them. Alasvu was quick-moving, impetuous, given to chattering away; Silish was the slow and stodgy tupe; Yanvusarran gave an impression of short temper; Djagaz seemed the most intellectual, and worked hardest with Avery. Lorenzen tried to follow the language lessons, without much success; they had progressed beyond the elementary level where he could have caught on, though Avery said communication was still a baffling problem.

"You should teach me what you already know, Ed," urged the astronomer. "Suppose something happened to you—where'd the rest of us be?"

"At worst, you could signal the aircar to come pick you up," said Avery.

"But dammit, I'm interested!"

"Okay, okay, I'll make up a vocabulary of the words I'm fairly certain of—but it won't help you much."

It didn't. All right, so you knew the names for grass, tree, star, run, walk, shoot. Where did you go from there? Avery used to sit by the campfire at night, talking and talking with Djagaz; the ruddy light burned off his face and gleamed in the inhuman eyes of the alien, their voices rose and fell in a purr and a rumble and a whistle, their hands moved in gestures—none of it made sense to Lorenzen.

Fernandez had brought his guitar along—inevitably, groaned Gummus-lugil—and liked to play and sing in the evenings. Alasvu produced a small four-stringed harp with a resonating board that gave its notes a shivery effect, and joined him. It was comical to hear them together, Alasvu butchering *La Cucaracha* or Fernandez trying to chord on the Rorvan scale. Gummus-lugil had a chessboard, and before long Silish had caught on and was giving him some competition. It was a peaceful, friendly sort of trip.

But the dark sense of its futility dogged Lorenzen. Sometimes he wished he had never come with the *Hudson,* wished he were back on Luna puttering with his instruments and photographic plates—all right, here was a new race, a different civilization, but what did it mean to man?

"We don't need more xenological data," he said to Thornton. "We need a planet."

The Martian raised his eyebrows. "Do you really think emigration will solve the population problem?" he asked. "You can't get rid of more than a few million people that way. Say a hundred million in the course of fifty years of continuous shuttle service—which somebody will have to finance, remember. New births will fill up the vacuum faster that that.''

"I know," said Lorenzen. "I've been through all the arguments before. It's something more—something psychological. Just the knowledge that there is a frontier, that a man with his back to the wall can still go make a fresh start, that any commoner has the chance to become his own boss—that'll make an enormous difference to Sol, too. It'll relieve a lot of unhealthy social pressures—change the whole attitude of man, turn it outward.''

"I wonder. Don't forget, some of the most ferocious wars in history were fought while the Americas were being opened and again when the planets were being settled.''

"Then isn't now. Mankind is sick of war. But he needs to find something new, something bigger than himself.''

"He needs to find God," said Thornton with a certain stiffness. "The last two centuries show how the Lord chastises a people who forget him. They won't escape by going to the stars.''

Lorenzen's face felt warm.

"I don't see why your kind is always embarrassed when I speak of religion," said Thornton. "I'm perfectly willing to discuss it on a reasonable basis, like any other subject.''

"We'd never agree," mumbled Lorenzen. "Waste of time.''

"You mean you would never listen. Well—" Thornton shrugged. "I've no great faith in all these colonization schemes, but it will be interesting to see what happens."

"I suppose . . . I suppose whatever comes, y-y-your Martian homes will be spared!" blurted Lorenzen.

"No. Not necessarily. The Lord may see fit to punish us too. But we'll live. We're a survivor type."

Lorenzen had to admit he was right there. Whether you agreed with the Dissenters or not, it was undeniable that they had worked and fought like heroes for their particular dream. It was they who seized control of the gaunt, barren, worn-out planet to which they had fled and made it blossom; it was their psalm-chanting armored batallions which had broken the Mongku Empire and fought Venus to a standstill. There was a vitality to the believer type—whether he called himself Christian, Zionist, Communist, or any of a hundred other faiths which had shaken history. It was too bad that the reasonable man didn't share that devotion. But then, he wouldn't be reasonable if he did.

He looked at the loping gray forms of the Rorvan. What dreams lay in those unhuman skulls? For what would they be willing to slave and kill and cheat and die?

Their planet?

CHAPTER X

MIGUEL FERNANDEZ was born in that province of
Latin America known as Uruguay. His family was
old and wealthy, and he had been one of the few
who always got enough to eat. And there had been
books, music, theaters, boats, horses; he had
played polo for his continent in the world matches
and sailed a yawl across the Atlantic. He had done
good stratigraphical work on Luna and Venus, had
laughed with many friends, loved many women,
and gone out to the stars with a song.

He died on Troas.

It came with cruel swiftness. After two weeks of
open prairie, they reached ground which rolled
slowly upward, toward the dim blue forms of
mountains peering over the horizon. It was a land
of long coarse grasses, thick clumps of trees, coldly rushing rivers; always the wind blew, and there
were many wings in the sky. Progress slowed
down a bit as the Rorvan circled to find the easiest
slopes, but you could still count on thirty kilometers a day or so. Avery said he'd asked how much
longer the journey would take, but had not under-
stood the answer, which seemed to be highly qual-
ified.

The party was strung out in a long line, scrambling over tumbled boulders. There was much life around here, tetrapteri broke cover with a flurry of all four wings, smaller animals bounded off in alarm, a distant herd of horned reptiles stopped and looked at the travelers with unblinking eyes. Lorenzen was walking near the front of the line, beside Alasvu, trying to improve his Rorvanian vocabulary by pointing to new objects. He saw a small bright-colored beast lying on a rock, sunning itself—rather like an oversized lizard—and indicated it.

"*Volanzu*," said the Rorvan. With practice, Lorenzen was getting so he could distinguish individual phonemes; formerly, all of them had sounded much alike to him.

"No—" It seemed odd to the astronomer that Avery still didn't know the words for "yes" and "no"; maybe the language didn't include them. But—"No," he said in English, "I know that word, it means 'stone.' I mean the lizard there." He stepped up close to the animal and pointed. It arched its back and hissed at him. The double sun made a jewel-play of its iridescent scales.

Alasvu hesitated, "*Shinarran*," he said at last, after peering closer. Lorenzen jotted it down in his notebook as he walked further.

A minute later, he heard Fernandez scream.

He whirled around. The geologist was already falling, and he saw the lizard clinging to the trouser leg. "*What the devil–*" He ran back, slipped on a rock, and got up in time to see Thornton grab the lizard by its neck and throw it to the ground and crush its head underfoot.

Then they were all crowding around Fernandez. He looked up at them out of tortured eyes. *"Hace frio–"* Thornton had slit his pants leg and they could see the fang marks and the purpling color around them.

"Poison—get that first-aid kit!" The Martian almost snarled it.

"Here—" Gently, Avery pushed him aside and knelt by Fernandez. As a psychman, he necessarily knew a good deal about medicine. His knife flashed, laying open the flesh.

Fernandez gasped. "I cannot breathe . . . *Madre de Dios,* I cannot breathe."

Avery bent to put his mouth to the wound, but straightened. "No use sucking it out, if it's already got to his chest." His voice was dull.

The Rorvan crowded helplessly about, looking as if they wanted to do something but not knowing what. Fernandez' eyes rolled up and they saw the breast lie suddenly quiet.

"It's paralyzed his breathing—artificial respiration—" Gummus-lugil's big hands reached out to roll the small man over.

"No." Avery was holding his pulse. "No use. His heart's stopped too."

Lorenzen stood very still. He had never seen a man die before. There was no dignity to it. Fernandez lay grotesquely sprawled, his face mottled bluish, a little drool still coming from his mouth. The wind slipped between the crowding men and ruffled his hair. Death was an unclean sight.

"Call the camp." Gummus-lugil fumbled for the radio on his back. "Call the camp, for God's sake. They've got means of reviving."

"Not with this stuff in him," said Avery. "Smells like prussic acid. The speed of it—! Good God, it must be all through his bloodstream by now."

They stood quiet then, for a long time.

Gummus-lugil called Hamilton and reported. The captain groaned. "The poor little devil! No, it's no use, we couldn't bring him back if he's been poisoned that thoroughly." It came out of the radio as a chatter of clicks. The Rorvan watched, and there was no reading their faces. Did they think it was some kind of ritual—that the humans thought a god was speaking to them?

"Ask him what to do," said Avery. "Tell him the Rorvan will still be going on and I, for one, am willing to follow them."

Decision came out of the machine "Bury him where he is and put up a marker. I don't think his religion would frown on that, under the circumstances. Is anyone ready to give up and come back here? The car can pick them up . . . No? Good. Carry on, then—and for the love of man, be more careful next time!"

It took a while to dig the grave with the few tools they had. The Rorvan helped, and afterward brought rocks to make the cairn. Avery looked at Thornton. "Would you like to say a few words?" he asked, very softly.

"If you wish," said the Martian. "But he wasn't of my faith, you know, and we haven't anyone of his along. I will only say that he was a good man."

Was it hypocrisy? wondered Lorenzen. Thornton, to whom Fernandez had been a papist; Gummus-lugil, who had cursed him for his noisiness; von Osten, who had called him a weakling and a fool; Avery, to whom Fernandez had only been one more factor to stabilize; he himself, who had never been particularly close to the man; even the Rorvan—here they stood around the grave, unspeaking save to voice a sense of loss. Was it only a meaningless form, or was it some recognition of the awesome stillness and the common destiny of all life? There was nothing more they could do for the dead flesh down under those rocks; did they wish they had done more while it lived?

By the time they were through, it was too late to travel further. They gathered dead branches, cut the sere grasses and bushes for a campfire, ate their evening meal and sat very quietly.

Djugaz and Avery went on with their language studies; von Osten rolled over and went grumpily to sleep; Thornton read his Bible by the dim red flicker of light; the other Rorvan murmured to each other, no more than a whisper. The fire crackled loudly; outside its wavering circle of light, you could see the moonlit world, and hear the wind talking in the trees. Now and then an animal howled, far off in the darkness, a long and lonely sound. It was not the night of Earth, not any night such as man had known—not with that double crescent huge in a cold starry heaven, not with those noises out there. A long way home, a long way for the soul of Miguel Fernandez to wander before it found the green dales of Earth.

Lorenzen murmured to himself, almost unconsciously, the ancient words of a Lyke Wake Dirge, and looked to the vague red-lit mound of the grave. Light and shadow wove across it, almost it seemed to stir, as if the one within had loved life too much to lie quiet now.

"This ae nighte, this ae nighte,
  Every nighte and alle,
Fire, and sleet, and candle-lighte,
  And Christe receive thye saule."

(And in the north lay eternal winter, and moon like icy rain on its glintering snows, the stars high and chill above the blinking glaciers, between the weird pale glimmers of aurora.)

"When thou from hence away art paste,
  Every nighte and alle,
  To Whinny-Muir thou comest at laste;
  And Christe receive thye saule.

"If ever thou gavest hosen and shoon,
  Every nighte and alle,
Sit thee down and put them on;
  And Christe receive thye saule.

"If hosen and shoon thou ne'er gavest name,
  Every nighte and alle,
The whinnes sall pricke thee to the bare bane;
  And Christe receive thye saule."

(What have we ever given each other, of kindness and help and love, in all the long nights of man? What can we ever give each other?)

Gummus-lugil moved over and sat heavily down beside him. "One down," he murmured. The weaving light etched the strong thrust of his face against darkness. "How many more?"

"It was the little things Hamilton was afraid of," said Lorenzen. "Not earthquakes and monsters and big-brained octopi, but the snakes and germs and poison plants. And he was right."

"A thing with cyanide in its fangs—what kind of metabolism is that? Can't have blood like we do." The engineer shivered. "It's cold tonight."

"It can be licked," said Lorenzen. "If that's all we have to fear, it isn't much."

"Oh, sure, sure. I've seen worse than this. It was just so goddammed—sudden. Why, you almost touched that thing yourself. I saw you."

"Yes—" Lorenzen felt sweat at the thought.

It struck him then. Alasvu had not warned him.

He held himself quiet, admitting the realization piece by piece into his mind, not daring to let it burst in all at once. Alasvu the Rorvan had not pulled him back from the lizard.

He looked across the fire to the small group of the aliens. They were in shadow, only their eyes glowing out of darkness. What were they thinking? What had they planned for these strangers from beyond the stars?

He wanted to tell Avery . . . no, let it ride for now. It could have been an accident. Maybe the lizards were rare, maybe this group of Rorvan had never seen one before either. Alasvu himself had been within centimeters of the fangs. The aliens couldn't be so stupid as to think they could murder every one of the humans and make it look like an accident!

But the *Da Gama* had never come home!

He forced down a shudder. He was tired, overwrought, his suspicions were childish and he knew Avery would label them as such. And if he told von Osten, the German would probably want to shoot all the Rorvan on the spot. Gummus-lugil and Thornton—well, not just yet, let him think and gather evidence before making a fool of himself.

He looked out into the western darkness. That was the way they were heading, into the mountains, into canyons and gorges and up thin slippery trails where anything could happen. And they couldn't turn back, not now, though they had no dimmest idea of what might be waiting for them.

"From Whinny-Muir when thou mayst passe,
  Every nighte and alle,
To Brigg o' Dread thou comest at laste,
  And Christe receive thye saule."

CHAPTER XI

THE LAND climbed rapidly, until they were scrambling through a wilderness of harsh rocky hills, between gaunt patches of shrub, and across brawling rivers whose cold was like teeth in their feet. It was hard to follow the Rorvan; their light graceful forms wove and bounded over the tumbled country; Lorenzen's breath was often dry in his throat as he gasped after them.

One evening, about a week after Fernandez' death, Hamilton's question clicked over the radio: "What the devil is wrong with your guides, anyway? You're arcing north again. Why haven't they led you straight to their home?"

Gummus-lugil looked surprised, but shouted the question to Avery. "Ask one of those hairy brutes why, will you? I'm sick of walking, myself."

"I have," said the psychman. "Didn't I tell you? But the answer seems to be another of those untranslatable things. I got an impression of dangerous territory which we have to skirt."

Gummus-lugil passed the reply on to Hamilton, who closed his sending with a click that might almost have been a grunt. The Turk sighed. "Not much we can do about it,'' he said.

Thornton chuckled. "Perhaps they mean to run us bow-legged and thus have us helpless," he suggested.

Von Osten clapped a hand to his rifle. "Dey lead us straight or—"

"No, take it easy, will you?" Avery spread his hands. "There isn't much we can do about it, I'm afraid. They *are* the guides."

Lorenzen scowled. It didn't ring true. More and more, the whole business was looking questionable.

He pulled out an aerial map of the territory and studied it for a long while. As far as he could see, there was nothing to distinguish the area which they were avoiding. Of course, there might be hostile tribes or something, but—

For every question he could raise, there was an answer. But all the answers were too *ad hoc*, they didn't fit into a consistent picture. All right, the poison lizard had been a species unfamiliar to the Rorvan, that much was pretty obvious; but why was it new to them? Any animal that formidable ought to have a pretty wide distribution—nor had the Rorvan come so terribly far from what seemed to be their own stamping grounds . . . Yes, the native language might be extremely difficult, but blast it!—a society, to be capable of the technology the Rorvan seemed to have, *had* to think and speak in terms which fitted the necessary concepts. When Western science was introduced to the Orient, the Chinese had generally talked and written about it in English or French because their own tongue wasn't suitable. So the Rorvan speech ought to have some structural similarity to the Indo-European group, enough so that Avery shouldn't be having all the trouble he claimed to be having . . .

For that matter, he was holding long conversations with Djugaz every night. He *said* they were language lessons, but—

Suppose they weren't?

Lorenzen sat quietly, letting the thought seep into his consciousness. He wanted to reject it. He liked Avery; and there was so little they could trust on this new world that if they couldn't even rely on each other—He must be getting paranoid.

Then there was still the *Da Gama,* a giant question mark floating somewhere out in space—

He lay in his sleeping bag, feeling the hardness of the ground beneath it, listening to the wind and the rushing river and the hooting of some unknown animal. His body was tired, but there were too many questions boiling up in his head for him to sleep. What had happened to the first expedition? Who had tried to sabotage the second? Why had it had such a heartbreaking series of minor difficulties before getting started? Why had Avery failed to mold its personnel into a unified team? Ill-assorted as they were (why?), it should still have been easy for a skilled psychman. Why were the Rorvan the only mammalian species encountered so far? Why didn't any of their artifacts show from the air? Why did they have such an incomprehensible language? Or did they? If not, why was Avery lying? Why had the Rorvan failed to recognize a danger which should be as well-known as a cobra on Earth? Their metabolism was enough like a man's so that it should be a menace to them too. Why were they doubling the length of the journey to their home? Why, why, why?

For every question there was an answer, either given direct by Avery or advanceable as a plausible hypothesis. But taken *in toto,* the answers violated Occam's principle; each explanation required a new entity, a new set of postulated circumstances. Wasn't there any unifying fact which would account for it all? Or was the whole thing really a jumbled mess of coincidences?

Silish was on guard, prowling around and around the dying fire. He was a noiseless flitting shadow, only the faint gleam of light on his eyes and his musket to give him away. Now and then he would look over the sleepers—and what was he thinking? What was he planning? He might hunt and sing and play chess with the humans, but they were more alien to him than the bacteria in his bloodstream. Did he really feel any sense of kinship, or was he party to some monstrous scheme which had already swallowed one ship and killed a man of the second?

Avery might not be lying, at that. He was a trustful, friendly little cuss. A psychman should know better, but then, he wasn't dealing with humans. Maybe the Rorvan had blinkered his eyes for some purpose of their own. Or had he been bribed somehow? But what could they buy him with?

Lorenzen turned, hungering for sleep. It wouldn't come. He had too much to think about, too much to be afraid of.

Resolution came at last. He couldn't tell anyone else what he suspected, not yet. There wasn't enough privacy in the group. No telling—maybe the Rorvan had picked up some English. Anyway, he had no proof, nothing but a hunch. *Take it easy, take it very slow and easy.*

But he had the beginnings of a Rorvan vocabulary. Suppose, without telling anyone, he tried to learn more. Mathematical analyses of data were out—he'd be seen performing those, except for what he could do in his head. But if you assumed that the language was basically inflected, its structure not too unlike the Aryan, by listening in on conversations, he could recognize words he knew and get some of the conjugations and declensions, new words would come from context. It wouldn't be easy, it would take time, but maybe he could do it. A lot of words could be learned by just asking, if they didn't suspect he was on the trail.

Eventually he was able to doze off.

CHAPTER XII

"IT ISS MURDER, I say!"

The wind whined about von Osten's words, blowing them raggedly from his beard. He stamped cold feet, and the ringing rock gave the noise back.

Around him and Thornton, mountains climbed steeply toward an ice-blue sky, their peaks sharp and white against it, their lower slopes tumbling in a dark cruelty of rock down into a gorge and a remote hurrying river. The land had climbed terrifically in the last few days, a great block of stone thrust up between the plains and the sea. Waking in the mornings, the travelers would find a thin layer of snow on the barren ground, and their breath smoked white from their nostrils. Hunting was poor, and some days there was little enough to eat; progress was a slow scramble over cliffs and crags, down and up knife-like ravines. It had been agreed to make camp for a couple of days and devote the time to foraging—getting enough food for the last push over the pass that lay white before them.

Thornton hefted his rifle and met the German's angry gaze with steady eyes. "The Rorvan could hardly have known that lizard would be right in our path," he said.

"No, but it vas a chance for dem to get rid of vun of us." Von Osten hunched his shoulders under the inadequate jacket. "Iss too many t'ings vat don't fit togedder. Dere iss somet'ing fake about dese aliens, and I say ve should down all but vun and beat de trut' out of him."

"Matter of language difficulty there," said Thornton dryly.

"Lengvitch, hah! Dey just don't vant us able to talk vit' dem. No lengvitch can be so hard like dey make out. Ven dey don't vant to answer a qvestion, dey just tell soft-head Avery, *'Versteh nicht'*, or dey jabber nonsense at him and he t'inks it iss some new trick of deir lengvitch. No, dey talk to him eassy enough if ve make dem vant to."

Von Osten reached out and tapped the Martian's bony chest. "And vy are dey leading us like dey do? I haff looked at our own maps. Vould be much qvicker and eassier to cross furt'er sout' and den follow de coastal lowlands nort'. I t'ink dis talk about skirting dangerous land is so much bull roar. I t'ink dey are giffing us a royal runaround."

Thornton shrugged. "Frankly, I suspect the same. But why approach me about it?"

"You iss de only vun I can trust. Avery iss a fool, Lorenzen iss a veakling, Gummus-lugil vould refuse to help just because it iss my idea. You and I can maybe do somet'ing."

"Hm—" Thornton rubbed his chin; the unshaven bristles felt scratchy. "Perhaps I can. But I don't want to rush into anything. Quite possibly the Rorvan intend to murder all of us. It is the easiest way to keep man off their planet. If the *Hudson* also fails to return, there will probably be no third expedition, and maybe the aliens suspect as much. But don't forget, they have to get rid of base camp too, which would be doubly alert if all of us disappeared. And the spaceship—how about it? How did they dispose of the *Da Gama?* It should have been in its orbit to this day, even if they lured the skeleton crew down somehow—"

Von Osten scowled. "I t'ink dey haff powers dey are not showing us. Maybe spaceships of deir own."

"While their warriors are armed with flintlocks? Don't be a fool!"

The German's sun-darkened face turned red. After a moment, he said quietly: "Please vatch your tongue. I vish to vork togedder vit' you, but not if you haff no manners . . . Haff you neffer t'ought maybe dose muskets are part of de game? If ve t'ought dey had not'ing better, it vould put us off our guard."

Thornton whistled. "In the name of the great Jehovah—!" Suddenly he turned. "Come on, we're supposed to be hunting."

"But my idea?"

"I want to think about it. I'll let you know."

They felt their way cautiously along the ledge that wound up the mountain face. Now and then they stopped to scan the harsh scene with field glasses. Dry snow scudded along the crags, but there was no sign of life. Thornton felt hunger gnawing in his belly, and suppressed the awareness. He had no business now complaining about the flesh.

If the Rorvan were *not* so primitive as they claimed to be, it opened up a whirl of nasty possibilities. If they were anywhere near the interplanetary level of technology, they would have been able to detect the *Hudson* as she approached; and in her equatorial orbit, she would make such frequent transits of Sister and the suns that the smallest telescope could spot her. Even if the Rorvan were only at the gunpowder stage, it was probable that they had telescopes. But if they were further along yet—then they could live underground, synthesizing their food; the custom might have grown up during a period of atomic wars. They could wipe out the camp and the ship with a couple of long-range guided missiles . . . Why hadn't they done so before? Maybe they wished to learn all they could first, and appearing in the guise of primitives was certainly a good way to disarm suspicion.

Thornton shook his head. "It still didn't quite make sense, there were too many loose ends and unanswerable questions. But he had to assume von Osten was essentially right. He dared not do otherwise. And if so—what to do? A quick blast with an automatic rifle, to wipe out the Rorvan in camp; maybe saving one for questioning. The commissars had taught humanity how to get truth out of any creature which could feel pain. A call to the camp, a quick return of all personnel to the *Hudson,* retreat into outer space—And then what? Troas would still be a mystery. He couldn't see the Solar Patrol making up a punitive force— but it would have to. It couldn't refrain, lest someday the Rorvan strike out of the sky at Earth.

Avery would scream to high heaven, pointing out that this was sheer unprovoked murder; he would doubtless lodge criminal charges when they got back to Sol. Lorenzen would, somewhat reluctantly, back him. Gummus-lugil was an uncertain quantity . . . How about Hamilton? The captain might put Thornton and von Osten in irons and stay here regardless; his caution never stood in the way of his duty as he saw it.

I have a duty too. A hard road to walk, O Lord.

It might be best to stage a mutiny, to gun down all those humans who would not string along. And that would certainly mean a trial when they got back to Sol, prison, psychiatrists turning his mind inside out . . . Thornton's wife and children would weep, alone in their home on Mars, and bear themselves with bitter pride in the face of their neighbors.

But the Rorvan were not human; the Noachian dominies doubted that any aliens even had souls, and in all events they were surely heathen . . .

Thornton knew what an anguished wrestling

with himself he must have before decision came. But already he thought he knew what the decision would be.

"Dere! Ofer dere!"

He lifted the field glasses at von Osten's whisper. High above them, peering over a massive jut of rock, was a horned head—game!

The two rifles cracked almost as one. The beast screamed and was gone. Furiously, Thornton began to run, leaping over stones and splits in the ledge. His breathing was fire in his lungs, but he had to catch that animal before it got away, he had to!

The upper ridge bulked in front of him. He scrambled, clawing himself fast to the rock. Von Osten grunted at his side, grabbing for handholds. It was like going over a fence. They reached the top.

And went over!

The moment was too swift for understanding. Thornton had a brief wild knowledge of falling, something smote him on the back and ripped his flesh open, he heard the angry whiz of a loose rock going past his ear, and then thunder and darkness came.

He awoke slowly, for a long time he was only aware of pain. Then vision cleared and he sat up, holding a head that seemed ready to split. "Von Osten," he groaned.

The German was already on his feet, looking dismayedly about him. "You iss all right?" he asked. His tone was perfunctory, he had checked the unconscious Martian and found nothing serious.

Thornton felt himself. There was a long shallow cut in his back, his head was painful and bleeding from the nose, and there were more bruises than he cared to count. But—"Yes, I think so."

Von Osten helped him to his feet. "Iss a curse on dis planet," he snarled. "It iss here only to murder men. I t'ink ve are caught in here."

Thornton looked around. The bluff they had climbed was the outer wall of a sort of pothole, about six meters deep and four wide; the animal they had shot had been on the further side of it, and by sheer ill luck they had gone over the bluff at exactly the wrong spot. The walls of the pit were nearly vertical, worn smooth by centuries of wind and frost and melting snow; a small hole in the bottom must lead to a channel that drained off the water.

He walked unsteadily about, examining the edges of the trap. Von Osten, who had suffered less, made several increasingly frantic attempts to climb out, but finally gave up. There was no way to do it without equipment they didn't have.

"Two more for de Rorvan," he said hoarsely.

"They couldn't have known—"

"Dey haff led us t'rough dangerous country. Chance has done for dem vat dey oddervise vould haff done for demselves. *Gott in Himmel!*" Von Osten shook his fists at the sky.

"Don't take the name of the Lord in vain." Thornton went to his knees and prayed. He didn't ask for help; whether he lived or died, that was God's will. He felt more composed when he was through.

"The others will come looking for us when we don't return tonight," he said. "They know approximately the route we followed."

"*Ja,* but iss a hell of a big territory to search, and ve vill not last very long in dis cold." Von Osten hugged himself and shivered.

"We'll have to fire shots at intervals, and take our chances of starting an avalanche. But we may as well wait a while with that, nobody will be coming this way for hours yet. Here, break out the first-aid kit and bandage me a little, will you?"

After that there was nothing to do but wait.

It grew colder when the blue sun set. Shadows began to fill the pit, and the air was like liquid. There was no breeze down here, but the men could hear the thin cold harrying of the wind up around the edge of the hole. They tried to exercise to keep warm, but there was no strength in them.

After the second sunset, they huddled together in an abysm of darkness, under the keen merciless blink of stars. Now and then they dozed, and woke with a shudder. They were only half conscious, time stretched horribly for them and the night was full of fleeting visions. Once Thornton thought he heard someone calling him, and started nearly awake; the voice rang hollowly down the long bare slopes, crying that he had sinned, and he knew it was not one of the searchers.

The long night wore on. When the first stealthy gray slipped across their little patch of heaven, they felt a dim surprise that they were still alive.

Now and then they curled stiff fingers around their guns and fired into the air. The echoes howled around them, and Thornton recalled the topography of this region with an effort. It was hard to think, but he suspected the surrounding cliffs would prevent sound from carrying very far. They might never be found, their bones might lie here till the double star was ashen.

The first sun climbed higher. They couldn't see it yet, but it melted the night's frost and a dozen bitter trickles of water ran down into the pit. Von Osten rubbed a frozen toe, trying to bring life back to it. Thornton sought to pray, but words wouldn't come, it was as if God had cursed and forgotten him.

Full sunlight was blazing into the pit when the Rorvan came. Thornton saw them peering over the edge and didn't recognize them at first, his mind was vague and stupid. Then knowledge came and he snapped to wakefulness with a jerk.

Von Osten spat an oath and hefted his rifle. *"Morderische Hund!"* Thornton knocked the weapon down just in time.

"You idiot! They're here to rescue us!"

"Are dey, now? Dey're here to see ve die!"

"And what good will it do us to shoot them?

Give me that gun, you devil!" They scuffled feebly. Three Rorvan stood on the pit's edge and
watched them. Wind ruffled their fur, but the
masked faces were utterly impassive and they said
nothing.

Thornton got the rifle away from von Osten and
looked up again. There was no sign of the aliens. It
was like a cold hand around his heart. So simple,
so easy. If the Rorvan meant them all to die, here
were two men murdered for them already. They
need only report that they had found no trace of
the missing ones.

So easy, so easy—Thornton felt his mind buckling. "Lord God of Hosts," he whispered between
his teeth, "smite them! Stay not Thy vengeance!"
And some sick corner of himself laughed and said
that maybe the Almighty was tired of man, maybe
these were his new chosen people who would
scourge a sinful humanity out of creation and
down into hell.

He felt death within himself, he was doomed to
freeze and die here, thirty thousand light years
from his home, and God had turned his face from
Joab Thornton. He bowed his head, feeling tears
harsh in his eyes. "Thy will be done."

And then the Rorvan were in sight again. They
had a rope, and one of them took a turn around his
body and the other was climbing down it into the
pit. Down to rescue the humans.

CHAPTER XIII

BEYOND THE PASS, there was another steep drop, cliffs falling terrifically into a remote glimmering sea. It reminded Lorenzen of parts of the California coast—the savage splendor of mountains, the grass and shrubs and low dark-leaved trees along their slopes, the broad white beach far below; but this range was bigger and sharper. Newer—he remembered Fernandez pointing out that the glacial era on Troas was due to a recent period of tectonic activity. The huge satellite probably made diastrophism here a more rapid process than on Earth. Lorenzen thought of the little geologist and his grave. He missed Miguel.

A good thing that Thornton and von Osten had been saved. He remembered a long talk he had had with the Martian afterward: Thornton had told of his plans, in short harsh sentences wrenched out by an inner need to confess to someone, and admitted he had been wrong. For if the Rorvan intended murder, why should they have rescued him? Lorenzen said nothing to anyone else about the conversation, but added the question to his own list.

Von Osten was still sullen and hostile to the aliens, but had obviously shelved his own schemes. Thornton, shaken by his experience, had swung the other way, to a trust of the Rorvan almost as great as Avery's seemed to be. The Martian was now brooding over the theological problem of whether or not they had souls; he felt they did, but how to prove it? Gummus-lugil slogged cheerfully and profanely along the interminable trail. Lorenzen felt very lonely these days.

He was making progress with the language. He could almost follow the talk of Avery and Djugaz, nearly enough to be sure that it was not just a lesson. The psychman remained blandly smiling, turning all questions with a deftness that left Lorenzen stuttering and incoherent. Yes, of course he was getting along with Djugaz, and the Rorvan was telling him some interesting things about his own race. No, he didn't want to take time out and teach Lorenzen what he knew; later, John, later, when we can all relax.

Almost, Lorenzen was ready to lay down the burden. Give it up, take Avery's word at face value, stop thinking and worrying and being afraid. There would be an answer to all questions in due time. It was no concern of his.

He stiffened himself and bent bleakly to the job. It did not occur to him how much he was changing himself, how little stubborn and aggressive he had been before this. Apart from his research, he had been like most men, content to let others do his thinking and deciding for him; he could never quite go back to that.

The climb down to the sea was grueling, but took only a couple of days. Once they were on the flat coastline, it was like a vacation. Avery said Djugaz had told him it was only a few more days to their goal.

At this point of the shoreline, the coastal plain hardly deserved that title: it narrowed to a kilometer-wide beach, a thin strip of grass and trees, and then the high rocky bluffs at the sheer foot of the mountain. The strand was also Californian, a great stretch of fine sand piled into tall dunes and scudding before the salt wind. But Earth had never seen a surf as furious as that which foamed and roared at its edge, nor a tide so swift and deep as the one which marched up almost the whole width of the beach twice a day. There didn't seem to be any game here, but the party could live off herbs and wild beans for a while.

Lorenzen felt a tautness rising within him as the kilometers fell behind. A few more days, and then—the answer? Or more questions?

Death guested them again before they reached an end of wandering.

The tide was coming in near the first sunset that day, when they came to a point where the hills fell directly into the sea. Bluffs and wind-gnawed boulders lay half-buried in the sand, making a low wall across their path; beyond, the beach curved inward, a long narrow loop at the foot of a ten-meter cliff, forming a bay. The water here was scored with the teeth of rocks thrusting out of its surface; a kilometer from the beach, the mouth of the bay was white violence where the sea thundered against a line of skerries.

Lorenzen paused on the top of the wall, looking uneasily ahead at the thin strip of sand. "That stuff is under water at high tide," he said. "And the tide's coming in."

"Not that fast," said Gummus-lugil. "It'll take less than half an hour to get across, and we won't even get our feet wet. Come on!" He jumped back down to the sand, and Lorenzen shrugged and followed. The Rorvan were already ahead of them, moving with the light rippling grace which had grown familiar in these weeks.

They were halfway across, hugging the foot of the cliff, when the sea broke in.

Lorenzen saw it as a sudden white curtain rising over the barrier. The roll of surf became a rising cannonade, ringing and screaming between the stones. He sprang back as the water level rose and rushed in across the beach.

A wave toppled over the outer skerries and came in with a blinding speed. Lorenzen yelled as its teeth closed around his knees. Another was on its back, green and white fury, spray exploded in his face and the sea got him around the hips. He fell, the water sheeted over his head, he rose with a howl and a fist seemed to batter him down again.

Rising, striking out wildly, he was whirled outward by the undertow. His boots dragged at him, yanking him beneath. The waters bellowed and tossed him back, against the white rush of surf at the cliff's edge.

Clawing for a hold in the churning water, he looked about him through half-blinded eyes. There, up ahead in the fury, a rock rising —He twisted, fighting to stay above water. Briefly, a Rorvan was whipped by him, he heard a dying scream and then the sea snarled up to shake the world and he went under again.

Up . . . over . . . strike, kick, reach—The slippery stone would not take his hands. A wave grabbed him and dashed him away—then back, over the rock, he closed his arms around something and hung on.

The water whooshed about him, he couldn't see or feel or think, he clung where he was and lay blind, deaf, dumb, half dead, only a barnacle will to survive kept him there.

And then it was over, the wrathful waters sucked back with a huge hollow roar. He fell waist-deep and scrambled for the wall cutting off the bay. Before he got there, the sea was coming in again, but he made it. A wave sloshed after him as he climbed the wall. Almost hysterically, he fled from it, collapsing on the grass above high-water mark. He lay there for a long time.

Presently strength and sanity returned. He got up and looked around him. The wind tossed smoking spindrift into his face, and the noise of the sea drowned his voice. But there were others, a group gathered, they stood mutely together and looked with wildness at each other. Human and Rorvan eyes met in a common horror.

Slowly, then, they took stock. Three missing—Gummus-lugil, Alasvu, Yanvusarran. Silish groaned, and it sounded like the anguish of a man. Lorenzen felt sick.

"Let's look around." Avery had to speak loud, but it came to their ears as a whisper under the anger of the sea. "They may be . . . alive . . . somewhere."

The tidal bore was receding, and von Osten climbed the wall and peered over the bay. Two forms stood on the opposite side and waved feebly at him. The German whopped. "Gummus-lugil and vun oder iss still alife! Dey lived!"

Silish narrowed his eyes, squinting across the sunset blaze that shone off the waters. "*Yu Yanvusarran.*" His head drooped.

"What did it?" breathed Avery. "What was it that hit us?"

"The p-p-place here is a goddammed trap," stuttered Lorenzen. "The c-conformation of the bay, a s-s-steep slope of the bottom . . . it makes th-th-the tide come in like all the legions of hell. We've got s-similar things on Earth . . . and here the t-t-tide is so much stronger—i-i-i-if we'd only known!"

"De Rorvan!" Von Osten's lips were white.

"Dey knew! It vas a plan to kill us all."

"D-don't be more of a fool than y-y-you can help," said Lorenzen. "It got one of them and nearly got the rest. It was an accident."

Von Osten looked at him in surprise, but shut up.

The tide dropped swiftly. They crossed the bay by twilight, to join Gummus-lugil and Alasvu. The Rorvan was collecting driftwood for a campfire, and the Turk was reporting the affair on his miraculously undamaged radio. There was no sign of Yanvusarran; he must have been swept out to sea, or maybe his corpse rolled at the foot of the barrier reef and waited for the fish.

The Rorvan set up a low keening. They stood in a line, holding their hands out to the water. Lorenzen listened to the funeral chant, and was able to translate most of it. *"He is gone, he is faded, he walks no more, no longer for him the winds and the light, but his* (memory?) *shall live within us . . ."* Their grief was genuine enough, thought the astronomer.

Darkness came, walling in the little circle of firelight. Most of the party slept, exhausted; one Rorvan guard prowled up and down, and Avery and Djugaz were sitting up talking as usual. Lorenzen stretched himself out near them and feigned sleep. Maybe tonight, he thought, he would get a clue. He hadn't been able to make much sense out of their talk before, but sometime soon he must catch on to the knack, and then his vocabulary would be large enough—

He had it!

Avery spoke, slowly and heavily: "I (unknown) not make-think others. Some not (unknown) laughing (?) with what I-say."

The trick was to cast what was heard into normal English, filling in the meanings of unfamiliar words from context, and to make the translation fast enough so that he didn't lose the reply. "I hope this does not make the others think (or: suspicious). Some are already not very happy with what I tell them."

Djugaz answered gravely: "Swiftly (unknown) theirs you, (unknown) time (?) to *Zurla* we-get see past shadow (?) they." Lorenzen's mind raced, unnaturally clear: "You must swiftly disarm their suspicions, lest when we get to the *Zurla* they see past the shadow (or: deception)."

"I do not think they will. How could they? And after all, I have the weight of authority (?), they will listen to me. At worst (?), that can be done to them which was done to the first expedition (?), but I hope (?) that will not be necessary. It is not a pleasant (?) thing to do."

A harsh flare of fanaticism: "If we must, then we must. There are larger issues (?) at stake than a few lives."

Avery sighed and rubbed his eyes like a man driven to immense weariness. "I know, There is no turning back. Even you do not realize how much is involved (?)." He looked up at the high cold radiance of the stars. "Perhaps (?) all of that—the entire universe (?) —all time and all space." There was a croak of pain in his voice. "It is too much for one man!"

"You must."

"Sometimes I am afraid—"

"I too. But it is more than our lives (?)."

Avery laughed without humor. "*You* think this is an enormous issue! I tell you, Djugaz, you do not begin to understand how much—"

"Perhaps not." Coldly: "But you depend (?) on me as much as I on you—possibly more. You will follow my lead (?) in this."

"Yes. Yes, I will."

Lorenzen could not follow the rest of the talk; it went into generalities, abstract concepts for which he had no words. But he'd heard enough! He lay in the sleeping bag and felt cold.

CHAPTER XIV

THE MOUNTAIN range swung suddenly inland, at the same time growing lower and gaining an easier slope. Here there were rolling grasslands, trees and meadows and running streams between the hills. The Rorvan hastened their steps.

Another of their race, armed and dressed much like themselves, met them. There were whistling cries of recognition; Djugaz and Silish ran up to him and conferred swiftly, then the newcomer nodded and ran off.

"He's going to spread the news," said Avery after a talk with Djugaz. "The village will want to welcome us. They're a pretty friendly people, these Rorvan."

"Hm." Gummus-lugil gave him a close look. "You seem to be kind of familiar with their language after all."

"Yes. In the last few days, I finally got the key to it, and everything fell together all at once. Fascinating semantics it's got. I'm still not an expert by any means, but I can understand ordinary conversation."

"So? Who are these boys with us, then?"

"They were a delegation to another town, returning home after a . . . business conference of some sort; I can't quite get the exact meaning there. They happened on us and realized pretty quickly what we must be. Their knowledge of astronomy is good, about like our eighteenth century, and Djugaz quickly grasped what I told him about the true structure of the universe—its size and so on."

Lorenzen couldn't refrain from asking: "Where are their observatories? How did they detect the finite speed of light? They could hardly use Römer's method in this system and—"

"I don't know yet." Avery looked annoyed. "Don't be so dogmatic, John. Does every science have to develop the same way ours did?"

Lorenzen shut up. No sense giving himself away—God, no! It could mean a knife between his ribs.

"Underground towns, as we suspected earlier," went on Avery. "That custom seems to have grown up in the past couple of thousand years, when the climate was colder than it is now. Originally, I suppose, it was merely because a dugout requires less building material and is easier to heat, but now it's become almost a matter of morality, like our taboo on public nudity."

"And dey haff farms underground, too?" Von Osten frowned, trying to understand.

"No, they never developed agriculture—so much of the wild vegetation is edible the year around. Then too, they have herds of grazing animals for meat, induced to remain in the vicinity by some means I don't yet comprehend. Djugaz gave me the word for it, but I can't find a corresponding concept in any human language.''

Alasvu was listening to the talk, his head cocked on one side, as if he knew what was being said. Doubtless he had the drift of it, thought Lorenzen. There was a wicked mirth in the amber eyes.

"It's wonderful that they were still able to become civilized," said Avery. "A gifted race . . . perhaps without original sin . . . Do you know how many of them there are?"

"Quite a large population, I gather—at least a hundred million, though none of our party knew the exact figure. This is just a small village, a hamlet, we're going to; but then, they don't have any really big cities like us, they spread out more uniformly.''

Lorenzen looked at the psychman. The weeks of wandering had leaned him down and burned his skin dark, but still there was nothing impressive to look at, still he was a small round man approaching middle age, soft-spoken, genial, everything about him said he was dull but steady, mildly benevolent, a little timid—And he was party to a scheme which juggled with the destiny of stars! There was some goal which made him so ruthless that the fate of two ships and the will of seven billion human beings was nothing. Lorenzen shrank a little closer to the stolid, comforting bulk of Gummus-lugil.

He'd just about have to let the Turk know, if no one else—

One of the mountains hemming in the eastern horizon thrust long roots out toward the sea. As the party approached one of these, it appeared as a low escarpment fronting a giant hill. The surrounding land was bare, tracked and trampled by many feet. Trees grew thickly before the cliff, some of them ancients almost three meters tall, and out of this grove the Rorvan began coming.

They moved quietly, saying little, none of the babbling excitement a human crowd would have shown. There must be some fifty or sixty of them, estimated Lorenzen, about equally divided between male and female. The latter were dressed in kilts and sandals; the four breasts were not very human looking, but gave the final proof that this race was mammalian. Some of the males carried muskets, the rest were unarmed. They closed in on the humans, in a friendly enough way. A purr of talk rose from them.

"How come no young?" asked Thornton.

Avery put the question to Djugaz, and replied after a moment: "The children all go into special ...crèches, I guess you'd call them. I gather the family here has a radically different structure and function from ours."

Pushing through the grove, the throng came to an entrance in the hill—a great artificial doorway, ten meters wide and three high. Lorenzen forced down a shudder as he walked through it—would he ever see sunlight again?

Thick columns of rammed earth supported a broad corridor running into the hill with many branches leading off to the sides. The air was cool and fresh, Lorenzen saw ventilator grilles in the walls. "Good pumps, then," commented Gummus-lugil. "And they use electricity." He nodded at the fluorescent tubes which lined walls and ceiling and gave a steady bluish light. "Their technology can't be entirely on an eighteenth-century level."

"You wouldn't expect it to be," said Avery. "A lot of engineering advance in our own history has been sheer accident. If the early researchers had investigated the Crookes tube more thoroughly, we might have had radio and radar before 1900."

The corridor was quiet, save for the murmur of the air blowers and the shuffle of many feet. It sloped gently downward for a good half kilometer. Glancing in the side tunnels, Lorenzen saw doorways presumably leading into rooms or suites.

The main passage opened on a great cubical cavern. This was lined with entrances screened off by tapestries that seemed to be of woven fiber. "Downtown," said Avery with a wry smile.

"They don't seem to have much artistic sense," said Lorenzen dubiously. The whole place had a depressingly barren air to it, neat and clean but without sign of decoration.

Djugaz said something and Avery translated: "This is quite a new settlement. They haven't had time to fix it up yet. It's partly a colony, partly a military post; I gather that the females fight as well as the males.''

"So dey are not united here?" rumbled von Osten.

"No, not quite. I've already learned that the continent is divided among several nations. Currently they're at peace and cooperating, but it wasn't so long ago that they had a terrific series of wars and the armies are still maintained at strength.''

The German's eyes gleamed. "Dey could maybe be played off against each oder.''

"I doubt it . . . even if we would be morally justified in such a course," said Avery. "I rather imagine they know as much about the *divide et impera* game as we do.''

One of the Rorvan made gestures at a pair of doorways, talking fast. "We're honored guests," said the psychman. "We're invited to make ourselves at home here.''

Inside, the apartments had the same bleak military look: each had two rooms and bath, furnished with a few low concrete couches and stools; that was obviously an easier material to work with than the native wood. But there was hot and cold running water, a flush system, a kind of soap. Apparently the village had a communal kitchen.

Avery disappeared for a while, talking with Djugaz and the villagers who seemed to be local leaders. Von Osten looked around the suite in which the other humans waited, and sighed gustily. 'Iss dis all ve haff come so far to see?''

''I'd like more of a look,'' said Thornton. ''Their apparatus, the general lay-out of the town, their daily lives—it should be interesting.''

The German grunted and sat down. ''To you, maybe. For me, I haff come t'irty t'ousand light-years and seen not'ing vort' de trip. Not efen a good fight at its end.''

Gummus-lugil took out his pipe and got it going. His face was moody. ''Yeah. I have to agree. Unless these Rorvan will actually let us settle here, the trip has been for nothing. We can't take over a planet from a hundred million well-armed natives with a high grasp of military principles. They could raise merry hell with us, just using what they have, and I'll bet they could soon be copying our own weapons too. Unless we could bluff them . . . but no, the bluff wouldn't last, they'd catch on fast enough and massacre the colonists.''

''Dey could be conquered!''

''At what expense? Spending how many lives? And all for the benefit of the few million people who could be shipped here. They don't command that many votes! Parliament would never agree.''

''Well . . . the Rorvan may still be persuaded—'' Thornton said it as if he didn't believe it himself. Nobody did. A race capable of building electric generators wasn't so stupid that it would allow several million aggressive aliens to settle on its home world. It could easily foresee the consequences.

Avery came back after an hour or so. He was wearing a poker face, but his voice sounded tired: "I've been talking with the local bosses, and gotten messages sent to the government of this nation—they have a few telegraph lines, its something new for them. That government will doubtless communicate with the others. We're asked to stick around for a while till they can send their scientists and so on to interview us."

"What's the chance of their letting people settle here?" asked Gummus-lugil.

Avery shrugged. "What do you think? It'll have to be officially decided, of course, but you already know the answer as well as I."

"Yeah. I guess I do." The engineer turned away. His shoulders slumped.

CHAPTER XV

THE REST of the day was spent in a guided tour of the village. There was quite a bit to see. Gummuslugil was especially interested in the power station, which he was told drew its energy from a hydroelectric plant in the mountains, and in the small but well-equipped chemical laboratory; von Osten took a good look at the arsenal, which included some large-sized mobile cannon firing explosive shells, a set of flame throwers, grenades, and a half-built experimental glider which ought to work when it was finished. Thornton leafed through some printed books and inquired, through Avery, about the state of Rorvan physics—which had apparently gotten as far as Maxwell's equations and was working on radio. Lorenzen tried hard to keep up a show of interest, and hoped he was succeeding. But every now and then one of the aliens gave him a sidelong look which might mean nothing or might mean death.

In the evening there was a banquet; the whole village gathered in a decorated mess hall for a series of excellently prepared dishes and the entertainment of musicians. The town commander made a mercifully short speech on the "hands-across-space" theme, and Avery replied in kind. Lorenzen faked boredom as well as he could, as if he didn't understand a word of it. Underneath, he was churning with worry. All that day the farce had been kept up. The Rorvan had asked the expected questions of Avery—about his race, its history, science, beliefs, intentions—well, that would fit in with the astronomer's deductions of the truth; the aliens would still have a normal curiosity about man. But why this solemn rigmarole of talks which presumably only Avery would understand? Was it for his, Lorenzen's, benefit—had Avery warned them that he might know more than he let on? And if so, how much of what he knew did Avery know he knew?

This was getting worse every minute; questions within questions. And what to do, what to do? Lorenzen glanced down the long bright table. The Rorvan were there in their Sunday best, barbaric splashes of color against the drab, soiled gray of the humans' hiking clothes—rank upon rank of them, face after face, each one mobile and smiling and completely unreadable to him. What did lie behind those golden eyes? Was he sitting at the table with the real masters of the universe? Self-appointed gods playing at humble peasant and soldier? When the Rorvan smiled, you could see the long fangs in their mouths.

It ended, finally, after a polite nightmare of hours. Lorenzen was sweating when he got up, and he couldn't keep his hands from trembling. Avery gave him a look which showed only sympathy—but what was *he* thinking? God in Heaven, was he even human? Surgical disguise, synthetic thing—what lay under the round bland mask of Avery's face?

"You don't look well, John," said the psychman.

"I feel . . . rather tired," mumbled Lorenzen. "I'll be all right after a good night's sleep." He yawned elaborately.

"Yes, of course. It has been rather a long day, hasn't it? Let's toddle bedwards."

The party broke up in murmuring, soft-footed knots of aliens. A guard of honor—or was it just a plain guard?—shouldered arms and marched behind the humans on the way to their apartments. They had two adjoining ones, and Avery himself had suggested that Lorenzen and Gummus-lugil should take one, the other three the remaining one. If they were to be here several days, that was a tactful measure to avoid a clash between the Turk and von Osten, but—

"Goodnight, boys . . . See you in the morning . . . 'Night . . . "

Lorenzen drew the curtain that shut his place off from the street. Inside, it was a barren cave, coldly lit by the fluoros in the ceiling. There was a great sudden quiet, this was not a human town with its restless life. Gummus-lugil spied a bottle on the table and reached for it with a delighted grin.

"Some of their wine —nice of them, and I could sure use a nightcap." He pulled out the stopper with a faint pop.

"Gimme that. I need it bad." Lorenzen almost had the bottle to his lips when he remembered. "No!"

"Huh?" Gummus-lugil's narrow black eyes blinked at him. "All right, then, hand it over here."

"God, no!" Lorenzen set the bottle down with a thud. "It might be drugged."

"Huh?" repeated the engineer. "You feel okay, John?"

"Yes." Lorenzen heard his own teeth clapping in his head. He stopped and drew a long shuddering breath. "Listen, Kemal. I've been hoping to get you alone. I want to . . . tell you something."

Gummus-lugil ran a hand through his coarse dark hair. His face grew wooden, but the eyes remained watchful. "Sure. Fire away."

"While I'm talking," said Lorenzen, "you better check your pistol and rifle. Make sure they're loaded."

"They are. But what—" Gummus-lugil started as Lorenzen flipped the curtain aside and looked out into the street. It was empty, utterly dead and silent in the chill electric radiance. Nothing stirred, no sound, no movement, it was as if the village slept. But somewhere there must be wakeful brains, thinking and thinking.

"Look here, John, we'd better let Ed have a look at you."

"I'm *not* sick!" Lorenzen whirled about and put his hands on the Turk's shoulders and shoved him to the bed with a strength he hadn't known was in him. "Goddammit, all I want you to do is listen to me. Then when you've heard me out, decide if I'm crazy or if we really are in a trap—the same trap that got the *Da Gama*."

Gummus-lugil hardly moved, but his mouth grew suddenly tight. "Talk all you want," he said, very quietly.

"All right. Hasn't anything struck you about these—Rorvan? Hasn't there been something strange about them, this whole time we've known them?"

"Well . . . well, yes, but you can't expect nonhumans to act like—"

"Sure. Sure, there's always been an answer, for every question we raised." Lorenzen was pacing up and down, his fists clenching and unclenching. Oddly, in this moment his stutter had left him. "But just think over the questions again. Consider the weirdness of it all.

"The Rorvan group, traveling on foot across a huge empty plain, just *happens* to find us. Improbable, isn't it? They are the dominant race, the intelligent ones, they are mammals, and there are no other mammals on this planet. An evolutionary biologist would wonder about that. They live underground and have no agriculture, seem to make no use of the surface at all except for hunting and herb-gathering. A moral code, we're told—but damn it, no morality lasts that doesn't make *some* sense, and this one is ridiculous. Our guides fail to recognize a type of venomous lizard which is probably widely distributed and certainly a menace to them; even if they personally never saw one before, they should surely have heard about, just as any American knows what a cobra is. Then, even worse, they get trapped by a tidal bore and lose one of their number—*within sixty kilometers of their own home!* They didn't know about the damned thing!

"I tell you, the Rorvan are fakes! They're playing a game! They're no more natives of this planet than we are!"

Silence. It was so complete a silence that Lorenzen could hear the remote humming of the village power station. Then his own heart began to beat so furiously that it drowned out all but Gummus-lugil's: "Judas priest! If you're right—"

"Keep your voice down! Of course I'm right! It's the only picture which fits all the facts. It explains, too, why we were taken the long way around to this place. They had to build it first! And when the 'scientists' and 'government representatives' arrive to greet us—they'll be from the Rorvan spaceship!"

Gummus-lugil shook his head, slowly and amazedly. "I never thought—"

"No. We were rushed along, with smooth, pat explanations every time we did pause to wonder.

That phony language barrier helped a lot too; we naturally shelved our questions—in our own minds as well—till they could be answered directly. It's not a difficult language at all. I've learned the basics of it myself, once I decided that it was *not* hard. When I first tried to study it, I was given a lot of confusing data—faked! There's no more variation in the name of an object, for instance, than there is in English or Turkish. Once I'd thrown out the false information—"

"But why? Whey are they doing this? What do they hope to gain?"

"The planet, of course. If we go home and report that there are highly civilized natives, Earth will lose interest in Troas and their own people can come here in droves. Then it'll be too late for us, they'll *have* the planet and we won't be able to get them off it."

Gummus-lugil stood up. There was a grimness in his face; he had changed his mind about a lot of things in a few minutes. "Good work, John! I'm pretty damn sure you're right. But . . . d'you think they intend to murder us?"

"No. They rescued Joab and Friedrich, remember, whom they could just as easily have left to die. I don't think they'll kill us unless they suspect we know the truth. Our negative report at home will be of more value to them than our disappearance."

"Why—" Gummus-lugil grinned, a savage

white flash of teeth in the broad swarthy face. "Then it's simple. We just string along with them till we get back to our camp and then tell—"

"But it's *not* that easy, Kemal! Avery is in cahoots with them!"

CHAPTER XVI

THIS TIME the engineer said nothing, but his hand dropped to the gun at his belt as he waited.

"Avery . . . little old Ed Avery," said Lorenzen. There was a sick laughter in him. "*He* faked those language data. He supplied most of those answers to our questions. He learned Rorvan and sat up late at night talking with them—" He sketched out the conversation on which he had eavesdropped.

"You mean the *Da Gama* case is . . . related to ours?" Gummus-lugil's voice was thick.

"It fits in, doesn't it? The first expedition disappears. The second endures a string of troubles which would have made anyone but a bunch of near-fanatics like the Institute's directors quit. The government helps recruit personnel for the trip, and we get the most badly selected, conflicting, inefficient crew which ever took a ship into space. Avery is along as psychman and does nothing to mitigate those conflicts. Avery is also in an official position, one of the advisors on whom Parliament and the people are coming to lean more and more . . . And when we bull through in spite of everything, the Rorvan show up. And if we come home and don't make a negative report on Troas—well, the *Da Gama* vanished!''

Sweat gleamed on their faces as they stood confronting each other. They were breathing hard, and Lorenzen was beginning to shake again.

''But the *government*—'' It was almost a groan from Gummus-lugil.

''Not the official government. Parliament operates in a goldfish bowl. But the psychocrats, the advisors, the quiet unassuming power behind the throne—they have men everywhere. One Patrol ship, manned entirely by men sworn to their service, would have been enough to take care of the *Da Gama*. Will be enough for us.''

''But why? In God's name, why?''

''I don't know. Maybe I'll never live to know. But you could imagine an older civilization than ours—maybe the Rorvan are the real bosses of the Galaxy, maybe the psychocrats on Earth are their tools, or maybe both are cat's-paws for some other planet. They don't want man in interstellar space.''

There was another silence while they thought of a billion suns and the great cold darknesses between.

''All right,'' said Gummus-lugil. ''What can we do? Now?''

''I don't know,'' said Lorenzen desolately. ''Maybe we should wait, play for time, till we can get Captain Hamilton alone and talk to him. But on the other hand, we may not be allowed time.''

"Yeah. Anything could happen, couldn't it? If somebody—something—learned what we know ...Or maybe the Rorvan won't give us a chance, maybe they'll decide not to risk our figuring things out on the way home and will blow up the works while Hamilton is still unsuspicious." Gummus-lugil looked at the radio set where it stood in a corner. "I doubt if we could call from here. There's enough metal in these caves to shield us off, probably. We'll have to go outside."

"All right." Lorenzen went over and picked up his rifle. "Now is as good a time as any, I guess." There were robomonitors at the camp set to ring an alarm and start recording when a call came from the portable set.

The astronomer peered out into the street again. Nothing moved—silence, graveyard stillness. Under the violent thudding of his heart, he wondered if they could go out and make their call and come back undetected.

But if not—that had to be risked. That, and a bullet in the belly, however frightened he was. His own sweat stank in his nostrils, it was hard to keep from shaking, but some jobs had to be done. It was more than the possession of Troas. The Solar System, all humankind, had to know who its secret masters were, or there could be no peace for John Lorenzen in all his remaining days.

Gummus-lugil thrust his arms through the shoulders straps of the transceiver and stood up, grunting. He had a rifle in one hand, and a knife stuck in his belt. The preliminaries were over, now they were playing for keeps.

They stepped out into the street. Their eyes wandered to the curtained entrance of the adjoining apartment—Avery was in there. It would have been good to have Thornton and von Osten along, but they couldn't risk waking the man or creature or thing who called himself Edward Avery.

Down the long row of doorways, their hushed footfalls seeming thunder-loud; out of the central cave, slowly upward through the silent empty tunnel to the open sky.

A Rorvan stepped out of a side tunnel. He had a musket, and it swung to cover them. The yellow eyes blazed with sudden alarm, and he rapped out the question: "Where are you going?"

Lorenzen checked himself just before answering: he wasn't supposed to know the language. He smiled, spreading his hands, and walked closer. The Rorvan's gun wavered. If they were unsuspecting guests—Then decision came, and he waved them back.

"Of course," whispered Gummus-lugil bitterly. "And tomorrow we'll be told it was for our own good, there are dangerous animals out there . . . Go on up to him, John. Don't act threatening, but give him an argument."

Lorenzen nodded. He approached till the musket was almost in his stomach. "Look," he said patiently, "we just want to take a walk. Anything wrong with that? All we want to do is take a stroll, and you're a flea-bitten son of an illegitimate alley cat.''

The guard snarled, ''No!'' and tried to thrust him back.

Then Gummus-lugil was behind Lorenzen. He reached out and grabbed the musket and twisted the barrel aside. Lorenzen's own hand followed, jerking the weapon loose and stepping aside. The Turk leaped forward, his fist going before him. There was a dull crack, and the Rorvan lurched back and fell. Gummus-lugil tumbled on top of him, getting hands on his throat.

After a moment: ''All right. Cut some pieces from his shirt—tie him up, gag him. Might be simpler to kill the bastard, but—''

In a minute they were again moving up the tunnel, fast. There had been little sound, no alarm. But at any moment, the whole cave might wake with a scream.

The end of the passage loomed before them, blue-black darkness and the pitiless brilliance of the Hercules stars. They burst out of it, and the trees were around them and the sky overhead and they heard the remote squall of a hunting animal.

''Over here—away from the cave—that damned sentry! Now the grease is in the fire, whatever we do.'' Gummus-lugil squatted under the low, massive bole of a tree and slipped off his radio set. His fingers were deft in the gloom, feeling for the controls. ''Got to warm it up—what'll we do when we've sent the call?''

"I don't know. Try to hide out somewhere—or maybe surrender." Lorenzen drew a shuddering breath. He wondered if the pounding of his heart could be heard.

The dial face of the transceiver glowed, a round eye in the shadows. Gummus-lugil slipped on his earphones and tapped the sender key a few times, experimentally. "Not quite hot yet."

An alarm went off, a high screaming note which went through Lorenzen like a sword. He sprang back, jerking his rifle up and sucking in a gasp of air. "My God, they've found that sentry."

"Or they have a hidden detector somewhere, set to whistle when we try calling base." Gummus-lugil cursed luridly.

Slim leaping forms were boiling up in the tunnel entrance, black against its light. A Rorvan voice howled above the yell of the siren: "Stop that! Stop that radio (?) or we will kill you!"

Gummus-lugil began tapping out his message.

Lorenzen ran away from him, zigzagging between the trees till he was several meters off. The wiry underbrush snagged at his ankles, he stumbled and cursed and crashed an elbow numbingly against a hidden branch. But the enemy's attention had to be drawn from the radio, Gummus-lugil had to live long enough to send the word. Lorenzen yelled defiantly. There was no time now to be frightened.

A dozen muskets cracked. He couldn't hear the hungry buzz of lead around his ears, but several slugs thudded into the tree behind which he stood. It was a heavy trunk forking into two main branches at one and a half meters' height; he rested his rifle in the crotch, squinting between the blur of leaves, and thumbed the weapon to automatic fire. The Rorvan sprang for him.

His gun spoke, a soft chatter, no betraying streaks of light. The indistinct mass of running shadows broke up. He heard them screaming raggedly, saw them topple, and even then felt the sorrow of it. *Djugaz, Alasvu, Silish, Menush, Sinarru, you were good comrades. You were my friends once.*

The Rorvan drew back, out of the grove and away from the silhouetting cave entrance. They'd circle around and close in; but *dit- dit-dah-dit, dah-dit-dah,* every second they lost betrayed them.

Something like a tommy gun began to stutter, throwing a sleet of white-hot tracers into the darkness under the trees. So now they were pulling out their real armory! Lorenzen shot back, blindly, and waited for death.

More of them came from underground. Lorenzen fired, forcing them back; but some must be getting past his curtain of lead. The gunstock was cool and hard against his cheek. He was dimly aware of dew wet and heavy underfoot. A glow in the sky said that Sister was rising above the eastern mountains.

Something blazed in the cave mouth. Lorenzen

saw a knot of Rorvan explode, falling and fleeing. Two figures loomed huge against the light— Thornton, von Osten, they'd heard the racket and come out to fight!

The German fired in the direction of the tracer stream. Suddenly it went out. Von Osten roared and moved away from the tunnel entrance. He wasn't quite fast enough. Lorenzen heard another metallic rattle. Von Osten spun on his heels, lifted his arms, and tumbled like a rag doll. Thornton flopped to the ground and wormed for the shadows.

The night was full of eyes and flying metal. The Rorvan had surrounded the grove and were shooting wildly into it, even as they crawled and zig-zagged their own way under its trees.

"John! Where are you?" The urgent whisper ran like a snake under the low gnarled branches.

"Over here, Kemal."

The Turk belly-crawled to Lorenzen's tree and stood up with his rifle poised. The first pale streaks of moonlight fell between the leaves and dappled his face. There was no sound of victory in his tones, no time for that, but he muttered quickly: "I got a message off. Not time for much of one, just that we were in trouble with the natives and they weren't really natives at all. Now what?"

"Now," said Lorenzen, "I guess we just stand them off as long as we can."

"Yeah. It'll take the boys at base a while to play back my message, and triangulate our exact position, and send some armed boats here. We won't last that long.''

Gunfire crackled to their right. A heavy form rose and burst into the grove, running fast. ''Over here!'' cried Lorenzen. ''Over here, Joab!'' He and Gummus-lugil fell to their stomachs as lead snapped after his voice.

The Martian, almost invisible in his black pajamas, eeled up to them. He was breathing hard, and a stray moonbeam turned his face chalky. ''Heard the noise . . . got up, saw you gone . . . Avery said stay there, but . . . Rorvan tried to stop us, we fought through them . . . Just a guess you were being attacked, but a right one . . . What's going on?''

Lorenzen didn't answer. He was leading a crawl away from their position, toward a spot of deeper shadow. Here several trees grew almost in a circle, forming a high barricade. They slipped between the trunks and stood up, leveling their rifles in three directions through the boughs.

Then the Rorvan charged, and for a moment it was all blaze and thunder, yelling and shooting, golden-eyed shadows rushing out of shadow and falling again. A couple of grenades were lobbed but exploded on the outside of the natural stockade. The Solarian rifles hammered, hosing explosive shells. Rorvan bullets wailed and thudded, other tommy guns were waking up, a storm of killing.

The charge broke and drew back, snarling in the

moonspattered darkness. A few wounded aliens crawled out of sight, a few dead lay emptily where they had fallen. There was a sharp reek of smoke in the chill windless air.

Stillness, for what seemed like many minutes. Then a human voice called out of the dark: "Will you parley?"

Avery's voice.

CHAPTER XVII

"ALL RIGHT," said Gummus-lugil. "Come alone."

The moon rose higher, and a long slant of light caught the psychman as he stepped from behind a tree. There was no sight of the Rorvan, no sound from them where they lay ringing in the place of siege. After the racket of battle, it was as if an immense hush had fallen over the world.

Avery walked up to the ring of trees and looked into the mouth of a rifle. "May I come inside?" he asked gently.

"Mmmm—yes, I guess so," said Gummus-lugil.

The psychman forced his body between two boles. Lorenzen's eyes were getting used to the darkness now, he could see Avery's face vaguely, and there was no mistaking the horror that wobbled in his voice. "What do you want?" asked the astronomer harshly.

"To find out if you've gone crazy, all of you— why you turned on your hosts, friendly natives—"

Gummus-lugil laughed sardonically. Thornton shrugged and murmured: "They didn't seem very

friendly when they killed Friedrich von Osten."
Lorenzen made the full answer:

"They aren't natives, and you know that as well
as I do. You ought to! Or are you really one of them
in disguise?"

"What do you mean?" cried Avery. "Are you
all gone lunatic?"

"Stow it," said Lorenzen wearily. In a few cold
words, he explained his conclusions. "And what
has happened since certainly bears me out," he
finished. "They detected our radio. They produced submachine guns as good as any at Sol. And
they tried to kill us before we could call base."

Thornton whistled, and then clamped his lips
thinly together. Avery nodded, with a great weariness. "All right," he said tonelessly. "What did
you tell the camp?"

"What I've told you."

"There wouldn't have been time. Not in Morse
code."

Lorenzen felt admiration for the brain behind
that pudgy face. "You win," he said. "But we did
get across that we were in trouble and that the
Rorvan are not natives. With that much of a clue,
Hamilton can put two and two together as well as
I."

"You might tell the Rorvan that," said
Thornton. "If they kill us, the boats from camp
should be prepared to—punish them."

Suddenly Avery was raging. He shook his fist,
standing there in the middle of them, and spat at

the shadowy ground. "You fools! You utter blind blundering idiots! Don't you realize—the Rorvan run the Galaxy! You've set yourselves up against the Galactic Empire!"

"I wondered about that," whispered Gummus-lugil.

"Call the camp again. Tell them to stay away from here. They wouldn't have a chance. The Rorvan science is ten thousand years ahead of ours." Avery's voice dropped, becoming calmer, but he spoke fast. "It may not be too late to repair the damage. If you'll help me flange up a story that will satisfy Hamilton, things can still be patched up. But Sol must never know her true status. I'll explain why later, to you three only. But move, now! Stop those boats!"

Almost, he had them. The whip-crack in his voice brought Gummus-lugil's rifle down and the Turk half turned, as if to go back to his radio. Thornton's long jaw sagged.

Then Lorenzen laughed. "A nice try, Ed," he said. "Damn nice. But it won't go over, you know."

"What are you talking about? I tell you, if those boats come here they'll be disintegrated, the Rorvan will have to wipe out the whole camp and the ship."

Lorenzen's mind felt unnaturally cold and clear, it was like the high chill heaven above him. His words came hard and fast: "If the Rorvan are that good, why didn't they just annihilate us with a disintegrator beam? Or jam our radio? Why did they go through all this clumsy deception in the first place? No, Ed, you're bluffing again." With an angry snap: "And now, before God, you can tell us the truth or get out of here!"

Something broke in Avery. It was indecent, watching the sudden sag in him, how he slumped over and dropped his eyes. Lorenzen was obscurely glad the light was so dim.

"The boats ought to be loading," said Thornton. "It won't take them many minutes to fly here."

Sister was well above the mountains now, her strange face turned to a blue-green crescent ringed in by a thousand frosty stars. A low little wind sighed through the grove and rustled the leaves. Out in the shadows, two Rorvan spoke together, a dull mutter of unhuman voices; and far off, the sea pulsed on a wide beach.

"All right," whispered Avery.

"It's some plan of your clique in the government at home, isn't it?" Lorenzen thrust relentlessly against the man's buckling resistance. "You were the boys responsible for the *Da Gama* and for all our troubles, weren't you? Tell me, did you hire the Rorvan for this job?"

"No. No, they just happened to be here when the *Hudson* came." Avery spoke so soft that it was hard to make him out. "Their home lies, oh, I guess ten thousand light-years from Sol; it's an Earthlike planet, and their civilization is at about the same stage as ours, technologically. They were also hunting worlds to colonize. This expedition found Troas and was investigating it when we showed up. They saw our ship transitting the moon as we went into orbit.

"They got alarmed, of course. They couldn't know who we were, or what we intended, or . . . anything. They moved their own big ship into an orbit normal to ours and further out; naturally, not looking for any such thing, none of us have spotted it. They camouflaged their spaceboats and their camp; that job was done before we'd gotten around to photographing this particular area. For a while they watched us from space as we set up our camp and began working. It wasn't hard to guess that our intentions were the same as theirs, but of course they wanted to be sure, they wanted to know all about us while betraying as little as possible about themselves. So they decided to pose as natives . . . The party which guided us here was set down a few kilometers from our camp, after its artifacts had been manufactured in their machine shop. It went in on foot."

"Nice idea," murmured Thornton. "The strategy is even brilliant. Naturally, we would show and tell much more to primitive natives than to alien spacemen who might be potential enemies or competitors."

"Meanwhile," resumed Avery, almost as if he hadn't heard, "the rest of them were making this fake village. A heroic labor, even with their ma-

chinery and atomic power to help. They figured
the presence of civilized natives—if we could be
fooled into believing that—might scare us off for
good. You guessed rightly, John. So did I, as I
studied their language back in camp. Little dis-
crepancies kept popping up, things for which a
psychman gets a kind of feel . . . I finally con-
fronted Djugaz with the evidence and told him I
wanted to help. Since then I've been working with
the Rorvan.''

''Why?'' Gummus-lugil's tones roughened.
''Goddam you, why?''

''I wanted to spare the *Hudson* the fate of the *Da
Gama*.''

Silence again. Then: ''Murdered, you mean?''
growled Thornton.

''No. No, let me explain.'' The flat, beaten
voice ran on, under the shadows and the distorted
moon. ''You know doctrine for a returning interstellar ship, one that's landed men on a new
planet. It calls the Patrol base on Ceres, Triton,
Ganymede, or Iapetus, whichever is closest,
makes a preliminary report, and gets clearance for
Earth. We knew the *Da Gama* would report to
Ceres, and we suspected it would report Troas
colonizable. So we took care to have Ceres Base
staffed with men loyal to us. When the ship returned and called, it was boarded and taken over.
But no one was hurt. You remember New Eden?
The very beautiful planet of Tau Ceti which has
civilized natives? We've made an arrangement

with them. The men of the *Da Gama* are there. It isn't prison, they're free to live as they wish, we've even provided women. But we don't want them back at Sol!''

''A lot of them had families,'' said Gummus-lugil.

''Somebody has to suffer a little in great causes. The families have been pensioned . . . But I still wanted to spare all of you even that much. I wanted to—well, I have my own wife and kids. I was chosen by lot to be psychman for this expedition, and was ready never to see my people again. Then this looked like a chance—we could have come home in the normal way, reported failure, Troas would have been forgotten.''

''All right,'' said Lorenzen. ''So the psychocrats want to keep man from colonizing. Before long, the economic failure of interstellar travel is going to keep him from the stars completely. Now tell us why.''

Avery looked up. His face was tortured, but a dim hope stirred in his tones. ''It's for the best,'' he said eagerly. ''I want you to work with me, fool Hamilton and the others when they arrive—we can talk about an unfortunate misunderstanding, a riot, some such thing—I tell you, the whole future of our race depends on it!''

''How?''

Avery looked higher, up to the cold glitter of the stars. ''Man isn't ready for such a step,'' he said quietly. ''Our race's knowledge has outstripped its wisdom before now, and we got the two-century hell from which we've just emerged. The psychodynamic men in government were opposed to the whole idea of interstellar travel. It's too late to stop that now, but we hope to choke it off by discouragement. In a thousand years, man may be ready for it. He isn't yet. He's not grown up enough.''

''That's your theory!'' snapped Gummus-lugil. ''Your brain-sick theory!''

''It is history, and the equations which interpret and explain and predict history. Science has finally gotten to a stage where man can control his own future, his own society; war, poverty, unrest, all the things which have merely happened, uncontrollably, like natural catastrophes, can be stopped. But first man, the entire race of man, has to mature; *every* individual must be sane, trained in critical thinking, in self-restraint. You can't change society overnight. It will take a thousand years of slow, subtle, secret direction—propaganda here, education there, the hidden interplay of economics and religion and technology—to evolve the culture we want. It won't be blind, greedy, pushing, ruthless animals; there will be restraint, and dignity, and contentment—there will be thought, everyone will think as naturally as he now breathes. *Then* we can go into the Galaxy!''

''Long time to wait,'' muttered Gummus-lugil.

''It is necessary, I tell you! Or do you want your

race to stay forever animal? We've expanded far enough physically; it's past time for us to start evolving mentally—spiritually, if you like. We . . . psychocrats . . . have a pretty good idea of the path to be followed, the slow directed evolution of society. We have the data, and we've set up a lot of the initial conditions out of which Utopia will evolve. Little things—but a university has been founded in England, and in another two centuries Europe will again be a full member of civilization; the balance of economic power is gradually shifting into Asia, India will become a leading part of the Union, the contemplative Hindu philosophy will tend to leaven the aggressiveness of Western man . . . We have it planned, I tell you. Not in detail, but we know where we're going."

"I think I see," murmured Lorenzen. The wind wove around his voice, and a moonbeam flitted across his eyes. "Interstellar travel would upset this."

"Yes, yes!" Avery was speaking easily now, his tones played on them, vibrating through the grove like prophecy. "Suppose men learn that Troas is habitable. The Rorvan can't compete, they haven't our talent for military organization—that's why they were bluffing, and if the bluff fails they'll bow out and go look for another planet. It'll change the whole attitude of man. Suddenly the psychic atmosphere will become another one.

"If desultory search turned up one useable planet in twenty years, then a fleet of hunters would almost guarantee one every four or five years—more territory then we will ever need. Men will realize they *can* emigrate after all. The orientation of society will change, outward instead of inward; there will be no halting that process.

"Our psychodynamic data won't be valid any longer, we'll be as much in the dark as anyone else. The rush of emigration will produce a turmoil which we couldn't possibly control, our created conditions will vanish and we won't be able to set up new ones. The colonists will tend to be elements which were malcontent at home, and many of them will be rather unfriendly to Sol's government for a long time to come—more trouble, more unpredictability, no way to direct it at all! Before long, the scale of human society will become so big as to be forever beyond control. The idea of a unified Galaxy is nonsense, if you stop to think about it; there isn't that much trade or intercourse of any sort. A million eccentric little civilizations will spring up and go their own ways.

"Interstellar exploration will be given a tremendous boost. Absolutely unpredictable new factors will be forever entering, to prohibit stability— alien planets, alien civilizations, new knowledge about the physical universe, mutations—

"And man will again be the victim of chance. There will be chaos and suffering, the rise and fall of whole cultures, war and oppression, from now till the end of time!"

He stopped for a little while, his words rolling

away into silence. The four of them stood unmoving, huddled together inside a ring of alien guns. It was as if they waited.

"All right," said Avery at last. "You have my answer. Now I ask for yours. Will you help me explain all this away; will you go back home and keep your mouths shut for the rest of your lives? It's asking a lot of you, I know—but can you face the future you have betrayed if you don't?"

CHAPTER XVIII

THEY STARED at each other. "You'll have to decide quickly," said the psychman. There was a sudden calm over him, he met their gaze and smiled a little in the wan half-light. "The boats will be here any minute now."

Gummus-lugil scuffed the ground with his boots. Misery twisted his face. Thornton sighed. It was Lorenzen who felt decision hard and sharp within himself, and who spoke.

"Ed," he asked, "do you know all this is true?"

"I've worked with it all my life, John."

"That isn't an answer. In fact, you've used more than your share of semantically loaded words tonight. I asked how certain your conclusions were about what will happen if man stays in the Solar System, and what if he doesn't."

"The first is a virtual certainty. We *know* how history can be made to go. Of course, you could always say what if a dark star crashes into our sun—but be reasonable!"

"Yet you say with one mouth that if man goes to the stars, his future is unpredictable and his future will be black."

Gummus-lugil and Thornton jerked their heads up to stare at Lorenzen.

"Unpredictable in detail," said Avery, with a ragged edge in his tone. "In general outlines, I can foresee—"

"Can you, now? I doubt it. In fact, I deny it altogether. Reality, the physical universe and all its possibilities, it's just too big to be included in any human theory. And if things go wrong somewhere in the Galaxy, there may well be other places where they go right, more right than you or anyone else could predict."

"I didn't say we should stay out of space forever, John. Only till we've learned restraint, and kindliness, and the difficult process of thinking."

"Till we've all become molded into the same pattern—*your* pattern!" said Lorenzen harshly. "I claim that man crawling into his own little shell to think pure thoughts and contemplate his navel is no longer man. I claim that with all our failures and all our sins, we've still done damn well for an animal that was running around in the jungle only two hundred lifetimes ago. I like man as he is, not man as a bunch of theorists thinks he ought to be. And one reason we've come as far as we have, is that nobody has ever forced the whole race into a copy of himself—we've always had variety, always had the rebel and the heretic. We need them!"

"Now you're getting emotional, John," said Avery.

"A neat, loaded answer, Ed, which dodges the

fact that this is an emotional issue. A matter of preference and belief. Personally, I believe that no small group has the right to impose its own will on everybody else. And that's what you were doing, you psychocrats—oh, very nice and gentlemanly, sure—but I wonder how lonesome the wives of the *Da Gama* men are!''

Lorenzen turned to the others. ''I vote for telling the truth, going out to the stars, and taking the consequences,'' he said. ''Good, bad, or most likely indifferent, I want to see what the consequences are, and I think most men do.''

Avery's eyes pleaded with the remaining two.

''I . . . I am with you, John,'' said Thornton. ''Men ought to be free.''

''I want that little farm,'' said Gummus-lugil. ''And if my great-great-great-grandson can't go find his own, then the race will've gone to hell and it's too damn bad for him.''

Avery turned from them, and they saw his tears.

''I'm sorry, Ed,'' whispered Lorenzen.

Now it was only to tell Hamilton and the rest of the crew. The *Hudson* would go home; she would not call the Patrol, but head for Earth and tell her story directly to its radios. Then it would be too late for suppression. The government would fall, there would be a new election, the psychocrats would be booted out of office. Lorenzen hoped some of them could return later; they were good men in their way and would be needed in the days to come. But it didn't matter much, one way or another, not when men were looking up again to the stars.

"I should ask the Rorvan to kill you," said Avery. His voice came thin and shaking as he wept. "I won't, but I should. You've sabotaged the real future of man, maybe the future of the entire universe. I hope you're pleased with yourselves!"

He stumbled from them, back into the forests. Lorenzen saw flitting shadows out in the night; the Rorvan were retreating. Back to their own spaceboats, he guessed. Maybe they'd take Avery with them, to hide till the anger of men had faded.

From afar he heard the nearing thunder of Hamilton's rockets.

Two men and how many aliens, as much thinking, feeling creature as they, had died, and a government and a dream would follow them, so that all men might own the sky. Had Avery been right after all?

Lorenzen knew bleakly that his last question would not be answered for a thousand years. There might never be an answer.

FRITZ LEIBER

06218	The Big Time	$1.25
30301	Green Millennium	$1.25
53330	Mindspider	$1.50
76110	Ships to the Stars	$1.50
79152	Swords Against Death	$1.25
79173	Swords and Deviltry	$1.50
79162	Swords Against Wizardry $1.25	
79182	Swords in the Mist	$1.25
79222	The Swords of Lankhmar $1.25	
95146	You're All Alone	95¢

Available wherever paperbacks are sold or use this coupon.